Spirit OF FAMILY

S.J SMALE

Trafford rev. 08/05/2019

 www.trafford.com

North America & international
toll-free: 1 888 232 4444 (USA & Canada)
fax: 812 355 4082

CONTENTS

There is an old saying that goes: 'You can choose your friends but you can't choose your family'.

I am very fortunate that the family I was born into is loving and very supportive. We may all be a wee bit whacky, but I thank my lucky stars for that quality as well.

The special, different and talented gifts that my family all possess gives us a lot of pleasure and is very helpful at times. Parties have always been a hoot for us. It seems our friends enjoy the different qualities in each of us.

DEDICATION

Mother is the glue to our family. Her kind heart and loving ways have been our building blocks sustaining us throughout our lives. She has taught us to respect and value what we have in life and to those we meet. Money was always tight but we learned to appreciate what we have and not envy those that have more.

Mother instructed us to use our gifts wisely and always for the good. Although she likes to keep her gifts and ours secret, we are very grateful for them and the ones we all are born with as well. Our gifts have helped to guide us through some very difficult times. Life is precious.

CHAPTER

It had been a very busy few weeks for Stella. Now that she had time to relax she decided to browse through some of the cases in her inbox. Other women may take a vacation or a trip to the spa for relaxation and rejuvenation, but for Stella she needed her mind busy delving into different scenarios to truly relax. Keeping her mind busy chased away any unpleasant thoughts such as her upcoming wedding which set her nerves on edge just to think about it.

A good juicy case was just the thing to keep her mind off that. She reached over and grabbed a few files out of her overflowing inbox and placed them on her desk in front of her. Rubbing her hands and grinning in anticipation she dove right into the first one.

Stella wasn't the kind of Private Investigator that took on spying on adulterous spouses. She figured if the wife didn't know the man she married was a sleazebag before they got married then it was her fault for wearing blinders.

Besides it's only too easy to find out for yourself if he or she has been fooling around. A simple check of the purse or wallet, a sniff of a strange cologne or perfume was a good start. Added to that the late nights and poor excuses. No, she would leave that kind of work for the money bleeding lawyers. Stella liked the more intriguing and strange cases that came across her desk. She'd always been one that loves putting puzzles together and solving mysteries.

She had just finished going through the first two and was reading the third one when her door to the office opened. Stella looked up and her breath caught in her lungs. 'The dragon lady' as she liked to refer to her accountant Naomi Hughes sauntered in.

Suddenly Stella's mind flashed back flicking through her memory trying to remember if she had all her paperwork in order.

Naomi Hughes was wise enough to keep the snicker to herself. There was nothing intimidating about her. She was a plain woman who wore comfortable plain clothes. The only thing extraordinary about her was her love for number crunching.

She didn't question the fear she brought to this tough kick-ass woman, but secretly enjoyed the thrill it gave her. This tall lanky red-head had more power in her little finger than she had in her whole body. It was simply invigorating to know she made her quake in her boots at the mere sight of her.

Naomi was smart enough to keep the glee out of her eyes as she smiled at her boss, sending her a demure hello. But she couldn't help a quiet laugh from popping out when she noticed the shamrock nailed to the wall above her table. She walked over and began to organize the table before fetching all the files she needed.

'God, where had the time gone,' Stella wracked her brain. 'It couldn't be time for her to do the books already. Was it?'

Sweat began to bead on her face as she watched Naomi meticulously go about her business.

That's how George found her as he walked in, wide eyed and sweating. He just couldn't help it; he bent over howling with laughter at her predicament. 'My God,' he thought to himself, 'nothing in this world could touch her, but here she was sitting quaking in her boots over this poor little creature that couldn't harm a fly.'

He was so caught up in the humor of the situation that he missed the fire building at his reaction behind her eyes. It was as red hot as her hair.

Naomi turned her head thinking she heard something sizzling in the air and caught the look in Stella's eyes.

Oh my, her heart fluttered. If this was the look she gave to all the criminals she caught, was it any wonder they'd spill out a confession. Her hand holding the first file for her inspection shook so bad she had to set it down.

George caught the look as well and decided it was definitely in his best interest in order to maintain his health that he'd better stifle the laughter immediately. He knew she was very sensitive about her uncontrollable reaction to her poor helpless accountant.

The laughter died away but it didn't leave his eyes as his long strides ate up the room walking over to her, and taking a huge leap of faith, he planted a kiss on her thinned lips. He was surprised his lips didn't burn with the heat coming from her. When he lifted his head he touched his lips just to make sure there was no damage or blistering.

"Good morning Miss Hughes," he glanced over to the nervous little woman, gracing her with a brilliant smile. It had the desired affect he knew it would. He was well aware of the charisma he exuded and the affect it had on women but he never let it go to his head. Instead he felt it was another tool in his arsenal.

Naomi blushed wildly from the unfamiliar sensations running through her body betraying her. She muttered a quick greeting back to him and forced herself to look away and try to focus on the job at hand. Her mind was reeling from that beautiful smile. Her heart was still fluttering wildly in her chest.

When he looked back at Stella, her lips were pursed with disgust at his obvious flirtation with her accountant. But at least the fire had banked from her eyes.

"Did you come here to get your kicks? Why aren't you in your own office?"

"The heads of departments meeting ended early so I thought I would come over and see the love of my life before my scheduled squad meeting." He ran his hand over her luxuriously long thick red hair.

Stella jerked her head away from under his hand. Displays of tender emotions in front of the 'dragon lady' were not to be tolerated. That little woman had enough power over her and she did not want to give her any more by letting her think she had another weak spot.

"Yeah, yeah, busy here," she ruffled the file she was reading before the two of them came in interrupting her peace.

"That's what I love about you Stella, you are such a romantic." He checked his watch and sighed. "As it happens I have to leave for my meeting. I really came by to remind you of our plans for dinner and the theater tonight." He chanced another light kiss.

"I didn't forget," she did. "Okay see you tonight." She waved her fingers at him not looking up.

When he left the office, Stella got back to picking out a case. She didn't see Naomi looking her way biting her lip.

"Um, Miss Blake?" Worry had her building her courage to ask her boss for a favour.

Stella looked up from the file she was reading and noticed a worried wrinkle forming on Naomi's brow.

"Naomi, you've been with me for some time now. I've told you, you can call me Stella. Now what's wrong Naomi? I know that look. Is Stanley in some kind of trouble?" Naomi never showed this kind of emotion except when it came to her brother.

"Okay, spill it Naomi. What's he done this time?"

Naomi blushed remembering how her brother's genius had put them all in danger before.

"Oh, Miss, Stella," she amended. "It's nothing like the last time. It's about the game he and his friends invented. You remember the game." She shuddered at the memory.

"I remember very well." It not only put him and his friends in danger but threatened to reveal her family secret. It also resulted in one of Naomi's brother's friends being murdered.

"I'm so sorry for that trouble and so are they. It is about the game but not in the same way." She rushed on fidgeting with her hands. "You see, he just got serve with papers suing him over the patent for the game."

"Someone else is taking credit for its invention?" Stella remembered the game and the genius that was put into creating it.

"No, he's not being sued for the invention of the video game but for the name. "The Perfect Crime."

"Then why not change the name?" Stella figured that would be the logical way to go.

"The game with that name is already in production."

"Okay, so who is suing him?"

"A Mr. Wilfred Herrington." Naomi brought out the legal paper and handed it to her.

Stella sat back shocked by the name. He was the Wizard that captured and held her sister captive nearly killing her. He put Gwen in a trance and if it wasn't for her and her ancestor Queen Ravena working together they would have both lost their loved ones.

Wilfred is Geoffrey Summerset's son. Geoffrey is a full grown powerful Warlock from Gobrath's side. He found some way to work with Gobrath to attempt killing the Queen's son, her sister and George. Wilfred used his father's ring to protect him. That ring was now safely hidden away. The last time she saw Wilfred, he was magically bound.

"Naomi, have either you or your brother personally contacted him?" She knew if he found a way to break the binding of his powers they were in grave danger.

"No, not yet. We've only been in contact with him through the lawyers."

"Okay, Naomi I want you to listen to me very carefully. Under no circumstances, absolutely no circumstances, are you to meet with him personally. Tell your brother to stay away from him. Let your lawyers handle it for now and I'll look into it."

She had to warn them but didn't want to scare them into doing something foolish.

"Oh, Stella, thank you. I know I must sound silly asking you to help with a legal matter, but Stanley is so upset over this."

"Not a problem Naomi. Just remember what I asked you to do. I cannot stress that strongly enough. I need your promise Naomi."

"We won't meet him, I promise." The weight was lifted off her shoulders and she got busy happily going over Stella's accounts. In Naomi's mind there was nothing Stella Blake couldn't do.

Stella couldn't keep her mind on the files she was flipping through. She told Naomi she was going out for some fresh air and left the office to head over to her mother's.

Just hearing the name of the Wizard had her worrying for the young genius and his sister. They had no knowledge of what Wilfred was and hearing that he is once again going after them through her accountant's brother was something she had to take some time to think about.

Stella knew that she had to tell George about this development, but she needed time to mull it over in her mind first. She also thought about Gwen and how she was going to take the news that this Wizard is coming at them again.

It has taken Gwen some time to get over the fact she nearly died. Although she was giving a good performance that she was fine and had bounced back from that situation. Stella wasn't sure and still worried over her mental health. Then she had to deal with the fact her office had been broken into and an important file removed. Gwen's confidence has been shaken and that was something else she had to deal with.

Gwen was always the sturdy steadfast one. That may be from her accepting from the very beginning what flowed in her veins. Stella always struggled with that and was still struggling to a point.

But deep down, Stella knew that Gwen was coping with the problem of having her clients not trusting her. For Gwen that was the biggest cross to bear. Her reputation as a psychologist was on shaky ground now and knowing a few of her clients felt they couldn't trust her to keep their sessions secure and secret, was a huge blow to her. To Gwen, her reputation meant everything to her.

She had worked so hard to build up her reputation and to have that ripped from her was a huge problem for her. Stella knew that people came to her for help and trusted her to do that and keep what they told her secret and confidential. It was going to take a long time to regain the trust of her patients again.

All Gwen wanted to do was to help others. She only used her gift to accomplish that feat. She never used it to gain anything from those that came to her. She would never use it to force her clients to stay with her.

CHAPTER
Two

As soon as she walked into Blake Manor she knew it was a big mistake not to call first. It sounded like a hen party coming from the kitchen. Stella had always hated hen parties. She knew how to give and hostess a party and how to conduct herself in a social setting but it didn't mean she had to like it. Give her a setting where she had to break down doors or wrestle a criminal to the ground and she was a happy little camper.

Some women liked girly things. She was never one of them. The term Tomboy was not something she would ever think to call herself. She simply liked solving puzzles and showing others that she is independent and can take care of herself. Where other girls liked to take ballet lessons, she was more into martial arts and proving herself on the gun-range. In her mind, more girls should take an interest in those things; they would give them the sense of being capable of taking care of and defending themselves. Unlike herself, most women depended on men to protect them and then cry out that they are not being treated equal. The word oxymoron came to her mind when she thought about those women.

Well, truth be told, she was never really given a chance to experience that girlie side. Being on the receiving end of constant bantering and teasing and then being shunned by all the school kids forced her to build a shell around her. She learned to only rely on herself throughout her school years. At that time she never felt she could go to her family for support or comfort. Only Maria was privy to most of her problems back then. It seemed that her mother and sister lived in a dream world most of the time, believing in fantasy.

Maria never tried to drum into her the strange stories her mother and sister insisted on telling her, trying their hardest to convince her they were true. She wiped her tears and gave her the warm comfort of soft arms to fall into. Truth be known, Stella was Maria's favourite, but she'd never own up to that. Stella also loved her cousin Morgana for her somewhat dour personality and support. Morgana too never pushed her mother's ideas on her. Stella loved the way she spoke her mind and never apologized for her unfiltered opinions. She looked upon her as a kind of role model for her.

Having to rely on herself through all those painful years allowed no room to experience the feminine side of herself. She grew up tough and self-reliant. Her mother did teach them both about art and the finer things in life and how to conduct themselves in a social setting. Gwen excelled in these lessons whereas Stella struggled but eventually, and a bit reluctantly, grudgingly, learned them over time.

All through her life she felt that she was alone and had to deal with problems by herself. That was proved each time she came to her family with those horrible experiences and was told to use what was in her to deal with it.

Stella insisted she had nothing inside her other's didn't and finally gave up hope that anyone in her family was willing to help her. Their insistence that she was other, just made her pull further away from them and more into herself. Because Maria didn't persist in her family's belief had Stella turning to her for all the times of trouble and stress.

When she walked into the mayhem that was going on in the kitchen, she noticed that her mother had asked cousin Morgana to visit. The large old oak wooden table was loaded down with swatches of materials, papers filled with lists and bridal books.

Stella cringed. She'd come on important business but the sight of all that had her trying to back out unnoticed. Too late, her mother had seen her come in.

Her mother, a shorter vision of herself came rushing over and gave her a hug and pulled her further into the room. Stella noticed everyone was there. Louise, Deb, Angela, Maria, Gwen, Gertrude and even Tempest were all oohing and awing over the different materials and plans. Feeling like a trapped animal, Stella reluctantly allowed her mother to drag her into the estrogen filled room.

"Oh Stella," her mother beamed. "Your timing is perfect. We were just discussing the guest list and need your input on that. I think we can handle everything else. Deb has some wonderful ideas."

There was a chorus of agreement. All Stella could see was a bunch of bobble heads bobbing up and down with silly grins painted on their faces. If she wasn't so scared to the bone about what they were actually doing she would have found the sight hilarious.

The thought of wedding filled her mind sending all reason to take wing and fly away. She melted into the nearest chair.

Maria fetched her a cup of hot tea immediately. Her ample body jiggling with suppressed laughter at Stella's reaction to the situation going on around her. She patted her shoulder as she handed her the cup.

Stella's reflexes were on automatic drive as she numbly took the cup. When her mind finally surfaced, she realized she couldn't just blurt out her reason for coming with three mortals in the room. Deb, Louise and Angela knew nothing about the family secret. Her mind raced to figure out a way to talk to her family without them around.

Knowing there was no way she could get her family alone at this time without hurting the feelings of the others, she decided her news would have to wait for another time. But it would have to be soon.

Gwen sensed something serious was bothering her sister and that it had nothing to do with wedding plans. She frowned over at her sister and was rewarded with a small shake of her head indicating to her that now was not the time to go into it. Gwen simply nodded signaling that she understood.

The rest of the women were too caught up in the plans circling around to notice the silent conversation between the sisters.

Stella relented enough to throw out some names she thought might want to attend her wedding. Most of her friends were either on the force or were acquainted through her business. She finished her tea and excused herself on the pretence of work.

Once outside the house she pulled out her phone and called George. After a quick encoded conversation that ensured he would meet with her after his meeting she headed back to her office.

Naomi was just finishing up when she entered the office.

"Well Stella, I'm happy to say all the paperwork is here and in perfect order. Keeping it that way makes my job easier, thank you."

Phew, Stella thought and found relief rolling off her like an avalanche making her almost giddy from it.

Naomi placed the last file away went over and picked up her purse. She glanced over at Stella. Her face blushing putting some colour into her normally bland complexion.

"I'll tell Stanley what you said and thank you again for helping."

"Naomi, I like Stanley. He's a good kid and that is all due to how you raised him like you have. I know it could not have been easy for either of you. I'll do what I can. Remember not to have any contact with Wilfred. When I have something I'll call you."

"Thank you Stella, we'll do everything you say." Naomi left the office feeling lighter than when she had come in.

Stella sat at her desk drumming her fingers on the desk. She was so worried that even the files on her desk held no interest for her now. She needed to talk to George.

It seemed he cut his meeting short as he walked in half an hour later. He knew that look on her face and it didn't bode well for good news. He went to her and rubbed his fingers over the worried lines on her brow. For her to look like this it had to be something to do with what they are.

"Who," was all he said.

"Wilfred Herrington." She answered.

"That can only mean that his binding has been lifted." He frowned. "He must have had help with that. He is too young to have figured it out this soon."

"How did you find out he was freed?" George's eyes went to steel.

Stella filled him in quickly on Naomi's problem. George listened intently and when she finished, he was still baffled not understanding the connection to Wilfred and the Hughes'.

Then it hit him. Geoffrey was going after the kids to get to him and Wilfred is his son. They must be working together. If Wilfred is unbound, that meant his father was unbound as well. If that is true they are all at danger again. The only saving grace is that neither had Geoffrey's ring.

"They want the ring." He seethed. "Have you told your family yet?"

"I went over to tell them but the house is full of both our families and friends planning our wedding." She shuddered at the thought.

"Darling I think we need to put our plans for tonight on hold and go there later and tell them."

"Yeah, won't that be the icing on their cake. Gwen sensed something when I was there but kept it to herself because of all the others that were there."

"Well then, she'll inform your family that something is off after the others leave. That should prepare them a little." He offered.

"There's really nothing more we can do until later. I'm needed back at the precinct and you can busy yourself picking out a case until tonight. It's all we can do until then my darling."

Stella knew he was right. But her nerves were on edge and would stay that way until they met and told the family.

When George left she flipped opened a file and tried to concentrate on it. This one involved industrial espionage. The Yamada Engine Company claimed vital details to their new engine design were being leaked to competitors. They claimed their new engine would revolutionize the automotive world.

According to the file each person responsible in the designing phase were fully screened and had worked with the company for many years. Nothing like this had ever happened to the company before. The plans never left the building and were locked in a safe at the end of each day.

Stella's interest was captured instantly. She began writing notes from the file deciding to take on the case. She put a call through to Mr. Yamada to inform him that she was willing to take it on. They made a date to meet the next day. Meanwhile she got started on a background check on the list of names he gave her over the phone of those who worked on the design.

She was so intent on her work that she didn't realize how long she was at it when George walked in. She blinked clearing her head from her research to discover the day was over.

George strode over and began rubbing her shoulders finding knots as big as baseballs. She must have been at this for hours, he thought, relieving and releasing the knots with his thumbs. He heard her moan gratefully under his steady massaging. Her eyes closed and she almost fell asleep, until she heard him whisper in her ear.

"We need to go to the Manor." George moved his head to lay a kiss on the back of her head that had him yelping for his efforts.

"God Almighty woman," he placed his hand over the pain in his face.

Her head had snapped up at the mention of her mother's home, connecting hard with his face.

Stella rubbed her head trying to chase away the stars swirling behind her eyes from the pain.

"Well it's your own damned fault. You almost put me to sleep then drop a bombshell on me to wake me up." She snarled.

"Forgive me for not thinking that kissing you is a contact sport." He snapped back rubbing his chin.

"Apology accepted," she smiled getting up from her chair. She went up on her toes to kiss his injured face and was surprised to see lust build quickly behind his eyes.

"Uh, uh," she wagged a finger at him, "business first, play time later."

On the drive over George feverishly hoped his blood would flow back up to his brain before they arrived at the Manor. The love of his life had the power to fill him with lust just by looking at her. It could be very disconcerting at times. Especially, it seems lately at all the wrong times. But he wouldn't change a thing about her. And this was a pain he was only too happy to bear.

Of course, Wanda had no idea they were coming. She couldn't see her daughter in her mind when she was physically close to George.

Their knock was answered by Maria. Her face lit up when she opened the door to them. She closed the door after them and went to tell Wanda her daughter was here.

When Wanda walked out of the parlor and turned down the hall to meet them, her smile faded. She knew only too well that look on her daughter's face. Trouble had come to them again.

The parlor wasn't the place for meetings in her home. After giving each a peck on the cheek she led them down the hall to the kitchen. It was not necessary to ask why they had come, she would hear the reason soon enough.

Stella was only worried about how the news was going to affect Gwen. Her encounter with this particular Wizard almost cost her, her life. Stella asked Maria to please call the rest of the family in.

George could feel how tense Stella was and sat next to her rubbing her arm for support. He was powerless within the walls of the Manor and could only offer human support for her here in this way.

It did not take long for Gwen and Morgana to come down and join them in the kitchen. It only took Gwen one look at her sister to know trouble was brewing. They took their seats while Maria busied herself making tea.

"Gwen, you need to brace yourself." She reached over and took her sister's hand.

Gwen instantly felt the fear running through Stella for her. It took her breath away. This is part of her gift and she really felt the fear now.

"What is it Stella?" she whooshed out. She was far too frightened to look inside her sister's mind at the moment.

"Wilfred Herrington," Stella tried to say the name softly and felt Gwen's fingers tighten on her fingers.

"He's found a way to undo the binding I put on him," George offered to the room full of very startled women. "He has surfaced and playing his games with the brother of Stella's accountant." George looked at her to take over.

Stella pried her hand out from the death grip her sister held it in. Flexing her fingers to see if anything was broke and glad to see the bones were all intact, she outlined everything Naomi told her.

"Gwen you must go far, far away." Wanda was afraid for her daughter.

"I will not run away like a dog with my tail between my legs mother." Gwen squared her shoulders. She was never one that looked for revenge but she was making an exception for this particular Wizard. Her eyes narrowed at the memory of what he did to her and she wanted payback.

"Gwen, GWEN," Stella had to raise her voice to get her sister's attention. "You must not go looking for him. I couldn't stand it if anything happened to you. George and I will handle this. I just wanted to warn you all to be on the alert and be prepared so he can't get at any of you."

"Stella, he took my will away. He held me in a trance with a knife ready to pierce my heart. You will not do this without me. Since that time I've had my reputation soiled. I need to know I can fight. You know I do."

Yes, the last case had her office broken into and a very important file was taken to use against Senator Ewing, one of her patient's. Stella knew that between being put in a trance and nearly killed and having her patients feel less than trusting to share with her their inner most secrets, she was going through a bad patch of low self-esteem right now.

Telling her she was no match for a Wizard would just make her feel even worse now. But she was no match for a Wizard. Her talents lay in her mind. It's true she can send out calming soothing waves and link minds, but how can that defend her against what a Wizard can do?

If it came to a fight, and she really hoped it didn't, she would have to find a way to make Gwen feel like a real participant in it.

Oh great, something else to worry about, she inwardly sighed.

"Gwen I know how you are feeling. I know what you have gone through and that you want a piece of him but you are simply not equipped to handle a Wizard," she put up her hand to stop her sister flying off the handle at her.

"If it comes down to dealing with him face to face, I'll try and find a way for you to be there and help in some way. Gwen this is the best I can offer. But only under one condition," she warned. "You have to promise that you will remain here under the protection of the Manor when you are not working."

Even while she talked to her sister, her mind was busy trying to figure out what this Wizard was up to. He would know where to get at Gwen but he didn't go for her, he went after Stanley instead by legal means. It wasn't adding up to her.

Gwen was getting fed up with always being forced to stay at the Manor, cowering, while her baby sister was allowed to go out and face the danger. Not this time, she vowed. And, if Stella didn't like it, that was just too bad. She would find a way on her own to deal with that deranged Wizard.

"No Stella, I will not be wrapped up in a cocoon again. If you will not let me help, I will find my own way to deal with him."

"Gwen, darling, please listen to reason. Stella is right you cannot take on a Wizard all by yourself." Wanda was frightened for her daughter.

"Stella is not the only one with gifts mother. I know I cannot pull pieces of the sun into my hands or any of the other fantastic things she can do, but I am not without gifts myself." She brushed her mother's arm away.

Stella could see how low her sister's self confidence had slipped. She was never the jealous type and she didn't think this stubbornness stemmed from that. She needed to prove she was still a strong woman and could handle her own affairs without her sister's or anyone's help.

"But Gwen," Wanda began to plead with her.

"No mom, she is right," Stella interrupted. "You do have gifts Gwen and they will most likely let you know if you are in danger again. If you won't stay here, then please use them and be on full alert. We are all thinking of the worse scenario and it may not even come to that."

Stella glanced around the room at the women she loved the most. She just could not get a handle on what this Wizard was up to.

"I don't understand. If he found a way to unbind his powers, then why didn't he come after us instead of going this route?"

"He could not undo the binding a Warlock put on him without help." George interjected. "He had to have help with that."

Stella whipped her head around to look at him. "Who could have helped him?"

"Another Warlock would be my best guess." He waited for it to click in.

"Another Warlock? But the only other Warlock we know of is his father Geoffrey Summerset and you bound his powers."

"Yes, I did not think he would find a way this soon, but then I never counted on him having a son either, a son who is a Wizard."

"George if he is freed, why hasn't he come after us?"

"My guess is that he does not have his ring and therefore won't attempt to go up against me without it."

"Do you think that is what is behind this? They are searching for a way to find it?"

"I know that would be my agenda had the situation been reversed."

That made sense to her. They were going about it in a human way to stay under their radar. Her tingle went into overdrive.

"Okay, it seems they will not use their magic until they find the ring. Mom," she glanced over at her mother. "Gwen will be perfectly safe and she will use her gifts as her own alarm system."

She could see the relief on all their faces. Forewarned is forearmed and as long as the ring remained hidden they could go about their business but with all their guards up.

Stella only hoped that the two miserable beings would keep to doing things the human way long enough for them to catch them.

She knew that this was going to be very hard for her family. They'd just recovered from the last encounter with them and now it seems that they were going to have to deal with them again.

Stella's real concern for now was her sister. Although she was showing signs of righteous anger towards them, she knew that her last encounter had taken a lot away from her emotionally.

Although it made her stomach roil, Stella needed to change the topic of conversation to get her mother to stop worrying over her eldest daughter. She brought up the topic of the wedding.

Just the mere mention of the wedding put a gleam in all the women's eyes, except for Stella. Her eyes showed total fear and that brought out giggles from her family.

She and George sat there and listened to all the venue ideas they'd come up with along with the meal and then trying to guess what Stella's wedding gown will look like.

Again she was asked if there was anyone she wanted to invite that she might have overlooked.

Stella's only friends were the ones she made at the Academy and on the Force. She had one or two in her line of work now as well. Thinking of their names shed some of the fear as she recalled each name and listed them by ticking them off on her fingers. She never noticed that George did not contribute to the guest list.

Now that the mood in the room changed to a happier one, Stella knew she could leave the women to continue on discussing her special day as her mother likes to call it.

The atmosphere lifted immediately in the kitchen as the women all began to chatter about the details they'd been working on. It surprised Stella to find out how much they already had planned. The venue for the reception and the flower arrangements for the wedding, were some of the details. She heard Morgana mention about the menu for the reception that still needed some tweaking.

She listened as they all began to talk about the outfits they all needed to purchase. This last topic seemed to have them all totally engaged and making plans to head out to buy the perfect one for each of them. Stella decided to head out before they got into all the accessories they were going to wear with their outfits. Stella knew her mind would explode if she sat there and listened to anymore of their chatter.

She did wonder how her family could all be engaged in this totally human event. For her, this was the scariest thing she's ever had to encounter before. Getting married was a new horror for her and she didn't know how to deal with it. Yes she loves George with all her heart but to marry him would mean that she could lose or give up a part of her independence. Stella didn't know if she could risk that, not after having to rely solely on herself all these years. She's never had to answer to anyone but herself and didn't know if she could do that now.

CHAPTER

Three

They left the Manor with the women chatting amongst themselves. They had a lot to go over. George felt it safer for Stella if he stayed with her tonight. He was not convinced that Wilfred would stick to human means for long. He remembered him being cocky and arrogant. Human means would soon bore him. Knowing she could take care of herself probably even better than he could did not lessen the feeling that he should stay close.

With Wilfred on her mind, Stella never gave it a thought when George made it clear he was going to stay the night with her. She'd gotten so used to him sharing her life and bed, that she went about preparing for bed still thinking about the danger that was facing them all again.

That night she had jumbled dreams. One had her searching for something; another had her in a tug of war with Gwen and then slipping into a dark fog losing her sense of direction. She listened to

Stanley and Naomi calling to her but she couldn't tell which direction the voices came from. She tossed and turned most of the night.

George woke a few times and saw she was having bad dreams, but her actions didn't alarm him or give him fear for her safety like the other times. He pulled her close to him and hoped that might bring her some comfort. At least these bad dreams didn't cause sweat to bead her skin or take her breath away. It seems that she was having what others call normal bad dreams.

Stella walked into Mr. Yamada's office the next day for her morning meeting with him. He greeted her politely shaking her hand then gesturing her to take a seat. Pete Yamada was old school Japanese. She was to be made to feel comfortable before beginning the business she was there to discuss with him.

He stood five feet seven inches with short thick black perfectly groomed hair. His face was round and clean shaven. The graceful slant to his brown eyes peeked through small round rimless glasses. His suit and tie were impeccable as were his manners.

Pete offered her some tea which she politely declined.

Now that the formalities were over they got down to business. Laying in perfect order on his desk were the files of the people she requested. Stella noticed the struggle going on under his façade of calmness by the slight twitch in the corner of his eye. Loyalty was everything to him and somewhere inside one or more of these files could hold the name or names of trusted employees breaching that trust.

They went over each file with him giving her his take on each person. It seemed they were all long time employees and up until now were thought to be very loyal. They were all married in good marriages and had families. The only times for any not showing up for work were illnesses and vacation times. There had been no whispers of discord from any of them or about them from their co-workers.

"I have to ask, Mr. Yamada why you would assume the leak came from one of these people? From everything I see and from what you have told me they seem dedicated and happy to work here."

"I too thought the same, but I cannot ignore the evidence. They are the only ones to have the knowledge about the new engine. It gives me no pleasure to know that those I have put my trust in could do such a thing.

"I have known these people for decades and feel they are more a family to me than employees. This is very disturbing to me Miss Blake, but who else could it possibly be if not one or more of these people?" He indicated the files before him.

Stella could see this was very hard for him. "You are sure that no other employee has seen the designs or have been in any discussions about them?"

"We have a very precise order in the way we do things here. Only these engineers are allowed to work on the designs and they work together in a secure area to ensure nothing is revealed outside that area. They are free in that area to discuss and compare notes. I assure you no one else has access. Other than me," he amended.

"Mr. Yamada I will have to look into their financial records and their personal lives. That means I will be invading their privacy without their knowledge."

"It pains me that this must be done, but I have no choice but to consent to this and hope that when this is over and it is found that they are not guilty of this offense, that they will understand the need for this action."

"I'll begin right away and keep you updated with my progress," she rose and extended her hand.

Pete Yamada rose from his seat when she did. He shook her offered hand then handed her the files.

Stella left the building feeling better now that she had something to keep her occupied to take her mind off her own family problems.

George stepped off the elevator and walked into his squad room on his way to his office. He glanced around at his detectives all busy at their desks. Some were talking to individuals seated in chairs beside their desks, others busy on computers digging for information and others answering the ringing phones. The smell of stale coffee and sweat permeated the room. The detectives all greeted him with a nod or mock saluted as he passed by them.

Seeing them all working hard, with or without him in the house made him proud. It was a good squad. He smiled on his way to his office and then frowned at the mountain of paperwork weighing heavy on his desk.

Mentally rolling up his sleeves, he sat down and got down to the business of digging his way through it. He knew he was good at separating work and personal problems.

Because right now nothing could be done about the personal problem he focused on work.

He split the work in half. He dealt with the request forms first. He declined or approved overtime, time off, requisitions for equipment needed, commendations and schedule testing for those detectives and officers wishing to advance to a higher grade. After all that was done he settled in to go over the cases his detectives were working on.

The morning flew by and he was half way through the cases when his phone rang. George checked his watch before answering the phone and noticed he'd missed lunch.

"Lieutenant Smale, homicide."

"George," Stella's voice was filled with controlled rage. "I think you better get over to Naomi's house ASAP." She hung up.

George went in hot, the blue light flashing on his dashboard and the sirens peeling. It only took him ten minutes to cross town. He pulled up behind Stella's car, shut off the siren and climbed out.

He saw Stanley standing shaking with his hands cuffed behind him with Sergeant Connelly standing guard next to him. When he glanced over to Stella she signaled directing his eyes to the body on the steps to the house.

Sergeant Connelly came to attention the moment he saw the Lieutenant. George looked around and saw that the area was cordoned off properly securing the crime scene. Once he was satisfied that everything was done correctly and by the book, he walked over to join Stella.

By the pallor of her skin he knew she could see the victim as he used to look when he was alive. "Have you talked to him?" he kept his voice down.

"Not yet, too many cops around but it does not look like he is going anywhere anytime soon."

"Tell me where he is and I'll get everyone away for a few minutes."

As soon as the area was cleared by George calling all the cops over to him for a short report from each, she walked up to the poor soul floating looking stunned.

"What's your name?" she kept her voice low and tried not to move her lips too much.

The spirit looked up from his body on the ground close to the steps leading up to Naomi's house. "Tony Weaver, can you tell me what's going on? Is this a dream? I think I'd like to wake up now."

"Sorry Tony, but you're not dreaming. What is the last thing you remember before looking down at yourself?"

"That's me? That doesn't look like me." He looked confused.

"We will talk about that later Tony, right now I need you to tell me what you remember and I need it fast."

"Um, sure. Well I was just returning a dish mom borrowed from Miss Hughes when this guy came out of nowhere. It kind of spooked me you know? The next thing I know I'm standing here looking at this poor kid."

"What did the guy look like?"

"Big, he was big with long black hair you know down to his shoulders and the bluest eyes I have ever seen. One minute he was here and then poof gone and then I saw the kid lying on the ground. Whoever messed this kid up wasn't fooling around. I mean I have never seen anything like it."

Stella realized he was still in denial not admitting that the kid was himself and yes whoever it was did quite a number on him. But then she had seen this kind of murder before and wasn't surprised that the sight of it still made her stomach roil.

"Hey I hope you can find out who did this to that poor kid but I'm sorry Miss, for some reason I feel I really have to go now."

With that said his form changed into a wispy thin cloud of vapour stretching out, appearing to be sucked up and was gone. Stella hoped Frank would take good care of him.

George kept his eye on her while the officers were reporting and knew the instant she was alone again. He dismissed the men to go back and continue their work then walked over to stand by her.

"He described a large man with long black hair and blue eyes. Somehow I really don't think Wilfred fits the bill."

"But Geoffrey does." His eyes went to steel. "A Wizard is not capable of this, but a Warlock is. It seems that father and son are definitely working together." It worried him that he had not sensed him.

Stella looked down at the body. Where the eyes had once been were now two blackened holes, smoke still streaming out of them. The gaping mouth revealed a missing tongue and the body looked as if every bone in it had been crushed.

He was innocent and had nothing to do with this problem but that did not stop a monster like Geoffrey. Humans meant nothing to him. She knew this was a warning to her, her family and George. A red-hot rage began to build in her. Her green eyes cast off sparks she was in no frame of mind to control. An innocent, she thought, an innocent was used to get his message across.

She vowed right there and then that he would pay for this.

Dr. Ballard, the top M.E. was called to the scene at George's request. When he arrived he greeted both Stella and George then went immediately over to the body and got down to work.

It took a long time as all crime scenes do before the police, detectives and forensic finish up. Dr. Ballard had the body bagged and ordered it loaded in the wagon.

He walked over to Stella and George; taking off his rubber gloves he shook his head.

"You get to see just about everything in my line of work. I have only seen something like this once before." He was reminding them of Terry Conrad and they both knew it.

He waited for them to say something, but when they remained silent he just shook his head.

"I could not find out what caused the damage that time. Let us hope I find it with this poor boy. His family needs answers, Lieutenants, even if those answers border the line." He quirked a brow at them and left them to follow the wagon back to the morgue.

"Stella, we may need someone like Dr. Ballard. In our line of work since what we are keeps popping up, he is going to become suspicious anyway. How much do you trust him?"

"More than anyone I know, human that is. And yes, I agree it would be good to have at least one human that understands and will help and understand the answers to awkward questions."

"Then let's go pay the good doctor a call as soon as we deal with Naomi."

Naomi was balled up on the small sofa in her small living room. Her face was tracked with the tears still running out. She rocked back and forth shaking her head in disbelief that anyone could possibly do something like what was done to her friend's child, or think her brother was capable of doing such a horrific vicious act on another human being.

"Oh God, oh God, oh God," she kept whimpering to no one in particular as she rocked back and forth in her seat.

George went in search of something to calm her nerves and left the comforting in Stella's capable hands.

When Stella sat next to her, her head snapped up. "Oh God Stella they took Stanley away. They think he did that. He didn't I know he didn't. He couldn't. It is just not in him to do that." She screamed waving frantic arms in the direction of the front door.

"They wouldn't let me stay with him. They said I had to go back inside. Stanley is out there all on his own. Oh God Stella, he's out there with that poor boy. He needs me Stella," She screamed at her.

Stella put her arms around her and held her shaking body tight to hers. Her body shook so hard, Stella feared her bones would break.

George walked in carrying a glass of sherry, the only alcohol he could find. He held it to her lips and helped her take a sip, then another. Not being a drinking woman, it soon had the desired effect. Her shaking lessened and she was able to hold the glass on her own. She gratefully looked over the rim at the both of them.

"Miss Hughes," George began in a quiet soothing voice. "I can assure you that Stanley will not be charged. They only cuffed him so he would not contaminate the scene. They have to take him in for questioning. He was understandably a little erratic from finding the body in such a condition; they felt they needed to restrain him so he would not further contaminate the crime scene." He explained again.

"Oh, oh that's good thank you," she attempted a smile. Then her eyes went wide again. "Did you see what they did to that poor boy?" She was on her feet in a flash and dashing to the bathroom where she proceeded to become violently sick.

Stella shook her head at George. 'No way was she going into that.' George was just as good a coward shaking his head too. They both waited until Naomi got herself back under control again.

"I'm so sorry," she said when she returned looking as white as a sheet.

Stella walked over to her and helped her into a chair. "Naomi there is no need to apologize. Anyone would react the same way under the same circumstances."

"No," Naomi said shakily. "Not anyone, just weaker people like myself. You would never lose control like I just did," Naomi shivered.

"Miss Hughes, you are not weak. I seem to recall seeing you causing a certain kick-ass Private Investigator we know to quake in her boots whenever you walk into her office," George tried for humour to calm her down.

That comment got a severe look from Stella. He knew she hated the way she reacts to her accountant. But her anger soon died away when she saw the effects his words brought out in Naomi. She did look calmer and her shaking was beginning to lessen now. 'But he would pay for his comments later,' she vowed.

They both waited while Naomi tried to get her shocked system back under some kind of control. Thinking of the scene she witnessed outside her home only had her shaking again. Naomi valiantly switched her thoughts to her poor brother and how he must be suffering. Now all she wanted to do was to go to him to comfort him.

CHAPTER

Four

It still took some time to get her calmed down enough to where they felt Naomi could be left safely on her own. The next step was a trip to the morgue. Stella was banking a lot of trust in the good doctor to not only believe what they were about to tell him but to keep their secret as well.

They found him masked and gowned humming as he worked on poor Tony Weaver. The tune was kind of catchy. Stella had not realized how much she missed working with Dr. Ballard. It brought back some good memories standing in the autopsy room watching him slice and dice with compassion, humming a tune.

"I noticed that neither of you two was very surprised at the vicious condition of this poor boy," he spoke as he worked. "It makes me wonder."

Stella caught the resentment carefully cloaked. It pulled at her not to have been upfront and honest with him before. But she had

26

to protect the family and still hoped it would be protected after their little chit chat with him.

George watched her reaction, ready to pull back from the reason they came. What he saw was a pang of guilt for keeping the good doctor out of the loop. He brushed his hand over her hair for support.

"Did you two come here for a reason or just want to hang out and watch. This is not a spectators sport." He was getting a little testy with the two of them.

"Well hanging out with you is always a hoot Doc, but no, we came here with a reason." Stella threw back. "We are going to need your full attention though."

"Then you will both have to wait. I will not leave this poor boy like this. I need to finish. Go grab a seat in my office until I'm done."

Stella knew his rage wasn't pointed at them but at the person who did this to Tony. He took his job seriously and always thought of the bodies that came before him as people, not just corpses to be sliced open for their evidentiary value. The bodies that came to him were people not just objects. They all had a life before coming to him. Their worth was in the lives they led and others they touched up until now and not the condition or weight of each organ he carefully removed and preserved for further testing. He treated each and everyone with the utmost dignity and respect.

George said nothing, only nodded his head and putting an arm around Stella, he guided her back out of the room to head down to Dr. Ballard's office. He saw the absolute dedication this Doctor was filled with and his respect for him rose up a few levels.

While they waited George poured them both a coffee from the Doc's coffee maker. They hashed over the best way to let him in.

"Stella, I know you trust him, but do you really think he will go along with what we're about to ask him to do?" George worried.

"George I don't know anyone that I'd trust more other than you." She seriously hoped she wasn't about to make a huge mistake. "He's a man of science, but he's also a man filled with integrity, ethics, and compassion. You saw how he was with that boy in there."

"I trust your judgment Stella," was all he was willing to commit to at the moment. "I agree that he is filled with compassion, but will he be able to handle what we are about to impart to him?" He worried after hearing the Doctor was all science and not hearing a word about religion.

"God, I hope so George. This is going to shake him up. There is no one in his field I respect more. His findings have always held up in court and no one has ever questioned his expertise before."

Stella knew this was going to be very hard for the good doctor. For as long as she'd known him, he relied on science for his findings. Science was everything to him. As long as she'd known him, she never even heard of him having a passing acquaintance with religion. As far as she knew science was his religion.

An hour later Dr. Ballard walked into his office. Without saying a word he poured himself a coffee and took it with him to sit behind his desk. Stella saw what it did to him to have to work on the boy. It was the one quality she admired him most for, his compassion.

He looked so tired.

"You know what happened to that boy." It was a statement not a question.

"Yes," George volunteered.

"It was the same thing done to young Mr. Conrad as well awhile back."

Another statement.

"Yes," George agreed again.

"Then I think it is damned well time you told me what is going on." Ballard demanded.

"Dr. Ballard," Stella started, "Do you believe in magic?"

He eyed her over the rim of his glasses that constantly slide down his nose. "Stella, I do not need a bunch of riddles. This is serious business."

"Doc, I am being serious."

He checked her expression for any hint of funny business and found none. In fact her face was dead serious.

"What the hell is this all about!" he demanded.

George touched Stella's arm showing her he would take over.

"First let me say that both Stella and I have the utmost respect for you. I have not known you as long as Stella has but I trust her when she says that we can trust you to keep what we are about to tell you absolutely confidential. Our conversation cannot be recorded by any means and we will rely on your confidentiality. Do we have your agreement on that?"

"What the hell is going on!" his face scowled. "First I tend to what I consider a most horrific deed done to that poor boy, a deed you tell me you know something about, and then you ask if I believe in magic. Then if that is not enough you insult me by questioning my confidentiality, my professional ethics?" His face turned red.

"We don't question your ethics Dr. Ballard," George charged ahead.

It isn't often that Stella seen him angry like this and never has his ethics ever been questioned. His reports always held up in court. He was the best in his field. She understood his righteous indignation. If he hadn't reacted like he did she would have thought she had made a mistake in trusting him with her secret.

"What we are about to explain to you is of the utmost secrecy," George continued. "Stella assures me that we can trust you not to record by any means or speak of this to anyone. Not your friends, family or even the family pet."

That had Dr. Ballard sitting up. His mind letting go of the insult he felt and veering off in another direction.

"Are you telling me that boy has something to do with classified information?" His brows pulled together.

George looked at Stella and saw they were of the same mind realizing the good doctor thought this was national security. Since he was not as familiar with the doctor as she was, he nodded for her to take over, feeling he would believe it more coming from her.

"Doc," she spoke softly. "We'd like you to think of this as classified in the highest sense, but it has nothing to do with any bureau. You have known me for a long time," she waited for him to agree. He nodded.

"You know I always did things by the book and followed procedure." He nodded again. "You also know that I solved a lot of cases quickly with next to no evidence." Now he frowned not liking where this was going.

"Doc please answer my question without getting angry, it is very important. Do you believe in magic?"

He puffed himself up at that question but kept his anger under control.

"Stella, I am a man of science. It is not what I do but who I am. I know some things cannot be explained no matter how much we try, but magic, I don't know."

"Okay we can work with that. Think of this as one of those times there are no rational explanations." Stella took a big breath rubbed her face before taking the plunge.

"You know of my mother's gift." She waited for his nod and continued when she got it, although his eyes looked skeptical. "My whole family has gifts, special gifts, other worldly gifts," she waited.

Dr. Ballard physically put space between them by leaning back in his chair. He was getting really uncomfortable and concerned where this conversation was going.

She continued, "George is also gifted in the same way. If we show you something, something that may shock you, you have to promise never to reveal it to anyone what you see."

"Wait," he did not know why but something inside him shouted at him to stop them now. "If as you say you are all gifted, which I am not buying, why are you telling me this now?"

George took over seeing how Stella was struggling with revealing the secret.

"Dr. Ballard, we feel it necessary because of the work we do and what we are to have a human we can trust on our side."

"What. . . what do you mean what you are and need a human? We are all humans for God's sake including the two of you." He flustered.

"Dr. Ballard do you agree or not to keep the secret we are willing to reveal to you?"

His mind was reeling at this strange behavior from them. How could two respected intelligent people think themselves not human for crying out loud? This is more than ridiculous.

"I don't like games, and Stella, frankly I am shocked that you would consent to be a party to this."

"ENOUGH," George's voice boomed out sending the doctor slamming further back in his chair, fear filling his eyes.

"Do you agree to our terms or not Dr. Ballard?" George demanded.

"I. . .I. . .,"

Stella watched the blood drain from his face. She rushed to him undoing his collar so he could breathe. She told George to fetch him some water. They helped him to settle back down. Stella felt she might have made a grave error in thinking she could count on her friend. When his colour came back and his breathing slowed to normal, they took their seats.

"Dr. Ballard, I'm sorry, it appears I have made a mistake in asking you for your help. George I think we should leave." She got up to go.

"Hold it, just wait," Dr. Ballard shook his head. He was still feeling the effects from the Lieutenant. "Just wait a damned minute. You cannot just walk in here talk about magic, summit me to whatever it was the Lieutenant just did then walk away saying I will not help. Just give me a minute, damn it, give me some time here."

Stella sat back down and waited. They both watched him trying to make sense out of it. She felt sorry for him knowing his science was not going to help him this time.

"Okay, as a scientist I pride myself on having an open mind. I agree not to disclose anything told to me here."

George was not as sure as Stella and he relayed that by the doubt in his eyes. She patted his arm giving him a small smile. She knew once Dr. Ballard gave his word that was that. She could trust him. He was an honourable man, a man of his word.

And she counted on that.

"Dr. Ballard please listen, just hear us out first and please don't panic. You are in no danger. We are not human," she heard him sucking in his breath. "We are products of two worlds. George is a Warlock from the Warlock world and I am a direct descendant from royalty from the Fairy world. We will give you a small demonstration to prove this."

"You are in no danger," she repeated.

She turned to George to go first. George held up his hand cupped it and after a few words, a fireball developed and grew. He held it for a moment and then sent it away with a few more words. The doctor's eyes went huge but he did not say anything. His mind kept telling him it was a trick of the mind. This has to be one of those magician tricks he saw on the television.

Stella stood up took a few steps back and called upon her heat. Her green eyes sparked, the wind grew and blew around her loosening her flaming hair as she rose inches off the floor. She held there for a moment and then slowly released the heat bringing her back down. The wind died away and she took her seat.

Dr. Ballard opened his mouth, closed it, opened, closed. Never in his life had he witnessed such abnormal power. He was literally speechless. This was not just a magician's trick on the mind. What he saw her do was impossible. There were no mirrors in his office or special effects to account for her floating in the air and shooting sparks from her eyes.

They knew it would take time for his scientific mind to stop trying to explain it away. This was magic. Magic cannot be scientifically proved or disproved. It simply was. Magic was simply magic. He could not dismiss what his eyes saw.

George got up to go to him. "Dr. Ballard, are you alright?" he saw him flinch. George backed away and took his seat again to wait.

"I'm having a little trouble processing this but yes I am alright." He finally managed to say.

Stella and George remained silent darting looks at each other while they waited for the Dr. to come to terms with what had just happened.

"I think I could use a stiff drink," he said after a lengthy pause. He got up on shaky legs went over to his glass door cabinet and took out a bottle and three glasses. He poured the drinks then sat down behind his desk again. He took a long pull of his drink.

"Well," he said shaking his head. "I cannot deny what I saw with my own eyes. I can't explain it either. What exactly is it you want me to do with this, whatever it was I just saw?"

Both Stella and George sighed out their relief.

"We don't need you to do anything with it Doc, except keep it secret." Stella smiled. "We are not the only ones in this world living among you. What was done to Tony was done by another Warlock. What we need from you now that you have agreed not to give away our secret is to be able to come to you and tell you if magic was used to set your mind at rest on your autopsies. And to be able to have a human we do not have to be secretive with.

"I know it's a lot to deal with right now, but will you be okay with this? Can we come to you if there is another situation like that poor boy?"

"Other worlds, it's just mind boggling. Of course our scientists believe there is life other than ours in the universe, but I do not think they meant this kind."

"Dr. Ballard." George interjected. "What we are has nothing to do with other planets in the universe. When we mention other worlds, we are talking about parallel Worlds, not galaxies. Can we rely on you not to give us away?"

"My mind is still trying to find a rational explanation, but I know in my heart there just isn't one. So that leaves me no choice but to believe my eyes. I cannot say right now that I'm okay with any of this but I will keep your secret and try to be open when you need to talk to me. It's the best I can offer right now.

"I have one question for the both of you though," he paused. "Given what you told me and what I just witnessed, have either of you done anything like what was done to that poor boy?"

His eyes narrow. He always thought he was a friend to Stella but after witnessing what took place in his office, he realized he did not know her at all. And that weighed heavily on him.

"Your mind can rest easy on that score Dr. as neither of us have committed such atrocities." George answered for them both. "The one who did this comes from the black sheep of my family. Our worlds have good and evil the same as the human world. And yes I say the Human World. We are parallel with two other Worlds. But we can assure you that we do not condone, nor commit such atrocities you have now witnessed twice." George told him.

"We appreciate the weight of the burden we have placed on you Dr. Ballard and you have our grateful thanks. I can tell you this; ever since Stella came into her full potential she has hated lying to you by not disclosing the true means of death to those you took care of. Having you on our side, so to speak, is a great burden off of her."

That brought back and restored some of the friendliness he felt toward her.

Stella pulled her hair back and tied it in its usual ponytail before she rose up to leave with George. She cast a backward glance at Dr. Ballard before stepping out of his office. Her eyes were filled with gratitude proving she was right in trusting him.

Timothy Ballard slumped back in his chair after they left. He didn't miss the look in Stella's eyes and was torn between his feelings for her before she broke this disturbing information to him. Now he just didn't know what to think of her or the new Lieutenant after witnessing what he showed him.

To him magic was just smoke and mirrors. It was simply tricks to amuse the public. He never really believed in magic before. His life has always been dedicated to science and reason, not carnival or parlor tricks.

But he saw what he saw and that disturbed him more than those two could possibly imagine. They put a deep crack in the safe world of science that he based his entire life and career on.

Now that he witnessed the talents the two of them displayed to him, his mind traveled down Stella's career when she was a member of the Force. Before the strange happenings in his office, he'd always thought of her as the brightest cop ever to grace the Blue Family of the Police Department.

Her reports were so detailed and factual, like a computer. She became the poster girl of the Force and up until now he was so proud of her. But after what just happened in his office, he began to wonder if all her cases were closed by being the best, or did she close them by what he witnessed right here. That thought left him feeling very ill and very disappointed. If she solved all those cases because of what she just showed him, he felt betrayed and that she played them all for fools.

Until Stella came to work on the Force, no one that he knew of, had ever had such success in solving cases before, or even rose up in rank as fast as she did. Until now he thought she was one of a kind and brilliant and that the Force was lucky to have her. But if it was this something they both showed him, then he felt sick thinking she tricked them all. He found his emotions were mixed with a sense of betrayal from her and shock from what he witnessed them both doing in his office.

Timothy gave his word and he never went back on that. Honour, ethics and his faith in science were all part of his makeup. Now he has a lot to think about and hopes to find some way for his scientific mind to come to terms with this new development.

CHAPTER
Five

As Stella and George predicted, they did not hold Stanley for long and he was back in the comfort of his home and in his sister's arms. Of course the one responsible for the crime would never be arrested for it, but at least Stanley was off the hook.

When they left the morgue George went back to his office and Stella went to hers, both hoping they made the right decision in letting the doctor in on their secret. They both agreed that they not tell the family about their conversation with the good doctor, not just yet anyways. They were both still concerned about how the good Doctor was going to deal with what they talked to him about. There was always their backup where they could erase from his memory what they showed him if he didn't comply and accept to keep this secret.

George had to trust Stella when she said that no matter what the Doctor decided in his mind, he would not give them away after giving his word. She knew him better and he simply has to trust her on this.

Of course he knows about Dr. Ballard's reputation in the Courtroom. His findings always held up, but he didn't really know anything personal about him. This is a lot of trust he's putting into Stella's hands.

Stella got busy running the financials on the names Pete Yamada gave her. She hunkered down knowing this was going to take a lot of time.

She jumped at the sound of her door opening blinking her eyes to get them to focus. Stella did not realize how long she had been staring at the computer. It surprised her that her office was almost dark. Time flew by without her noticing and she had not even gotten through half the people on her list. But then she knew this part of her job took the longest.

George flicked the light on and strode over to her. Lust began to build in him seeing the glazed look in her eyes from too much time spent on the computer. She caught the look in his and it started a slow heat building in her center. Now the glaze in her eyes was for a different reason.

He gently stroked her cheek watching the heat build in her. She stood up wrapped her arms around him and leaned in and up to press her lips on his. She ran her tongue over his lips, opening them and dove in to take her fill. Their tongues danced sending shivers through them both.

He held one hand firmly at the back of her head to keep her mouth on his while the other slid down to relieve her of her holster. Once she was disarmed he began to slowly undo the buttons on her shirt slipping it off her then sliding his hand to cup her breast drinking in her moan. He knew she was already wet and ready when he unbuttoned her slacks letting them pool at her feet. His fingers ran along the top of the lace covering her. She went limp in his arms.

Heat building from them both had sparks shooting out as they rose together in the air. He removed the last barrier she wore and drove his fingers hard in her sending her crying out on the first crest. His needs were blissfully throbbing feeling her erupt in his hand.

Stella's hands frantically tore at his clothes. She needed the feel of his skin next to hers. When he was freed she took him in a firm grasp almost undoing him. She worked him with all the urgency her body was reeling with.

It was only with herculean strength that he held on not giving into the enormous urge filling him to let go. When she finally let go to roam her hands over his muscles he plunged in and swallowed her cry as she soared over again. He held on afraid to move lest he lose control. Then slowly, ever so slowly he began to stroke her in a slow rhythm to send her back up again.

Sweat beaded from the both of them, their bodies soaked in it. He began to speed up as she joined in the rhythm. Their wet sweaty bodies slapped against each other feeding the frenzy in them both. He felt her reaching the top of the crest and let go emptying himself as he followed her up and over the edge.

They drifted slowly down pooling on the floor. The only sound in the room was the labored breathing from two bodies desperate for oxygen. George slid off her and lay spent beside her.

"I swear I'm going to line this floor with mattress material," she gasped out.

He only had enough strength to let out a weak chuckle.

When she turned her head to look at him, she saw the smile plastered on his face. The idea of a crew of construction workers unable to wipe that smile off made her laugh. She rolled over and crawled to the steps leading to her quarters. This time she didn't wait for him, but crawled up them and headed slowly towards the kitchen.

Stella was just filling the second glass with water when she turned around at the sound of him coming into the room. She marveled at his strength when she saw his hands were filled with their discarded clothing. She handed him his glass and stood there gulping hers down.

When their thirst was finally quenched she took stalk of their condition. "God we're a mess. I need a shower."

"You look beautiful," his smile widened.

Stella snorted and left him to go take her shower. He joined her after a few minutes and sparks flew around them once again.

Snuggled next to him in bed, Stella wondered if she made a mistake in telling Dr. Ballard about them.

"I hope we didn't make a mistake," she yawned.

George knew where her mind was going. "I trust him Stella because you trust him. I think having him know will take some pressure off of us. He just needs time to adjust to it." George kissed her head and felt her drift off to sleep. Hoping he was right, it took him longer to shut his mind off and follow her into oblivion.

A sound had them both snap awake at the same time. George was never unarmed and really she wasn't either, but Stella quickly slid out of bed silently to retrieve her gun. By the time she had it, George was waiting by the door for her. He lifted a brow at her choice of weapon and watched her shrug.

Stella would never let him take lead so he followed close behind her, his hands ready. Neither of them thought twice about roaming the house butt naked, except for the gun. The sound was coming from her office. Stella glanced back at George.

"I locked up before I came into the kitchen," he whispered in her ear.

She nodded and crept slowly towards the door separating her office from her home. Through the door they heard sounds of drawers being opened and papers being rifled through. Whoever was in there was either new at burglary or wasn't worried about being caught. No self respecting burglar would make so much noise. It worried Stella that her 'tingle' alarm wasn't going off.

She grabbed the door knob and mouthed to George to make a light when she opened it. Putting up her hand she counted down from three with her fingers and yanked the door open. George produced a light and they heard a scream.

They both rushed in, Stella pointing her gun at the culprit. George flicked on the light switch, dousing his at the same time.

Both of them still butt naked.

They found themselves facing a very scared very young man with his hands in one of the file drawers. She saw his eyes dart from them to the door.

"Don't even think about it," Stella raised her gun to point at his chest.

He was terrified by the gun but shocked at the sight of seeing two naked bodies. His Adam's apple bobbled up and down in his attempt to swallow.

"George, I have a pair of cuffs in the bedroom. Would you mind getting them for me?" Stella never took her eyes or her gun off the young man.

George laughed shaking his head at the stupidity of this young criminal. He left her there knowing she was in no real danger from him and fetched the cuffs. He also took time to get a robe for each of them to put on.

When he was cuffed and they were semi dressed, she ordered the young lad to sit.

"Young man," George snickered. "You could not have picked the worst house to break into if you tried. Do you know who I am?"

"I don't give a damn who you are. I ain't sayin nothin." His voice trembled giving away his youth.

From the use of his grammar, Stella realized whatever education he managed to get was wasted on him.

"Well for your information I am Lieutenant Smale of the Homicide division in the police department." George cocked his eyebrow at him. "And you don't have to say anything since we caught you red handed."

"I wasn't told no cop lived here." His eyes went huge, his Adam's apple bobbing again.

"So who were you told lived here then?" George's voice went deceptively calm.

"Some dumb ass P.I. And I ain't killed no one neither." He lifted his chin showing some of his cockiness.

"Well now, I'm the dumb ass P.I. that just caught your ass in the act of a B&E and burglary. But from where I'm standing you look like the dumb ass." Stella gave him a feral sneer that sent shivers up and down his spine.

"Who are you and what were you looking for?" She demanded.

He was caught and he knew it. Having a cop in the house was not part of the deal. If it was just her here he might have been able to talk his way out but a cop meant he was going down. Why wasn't he told a cop lived here too?

His mind was racing trying to find a way out of the mess. Maybe since nothing was broke and nobody was hurt he could talk his way out.

"Look I didn't break nothin and nobody got hurt. What do you say we just forget about this?" He tried for a smile but didn't quite pull it off.

"Oh so you break into my home and now you want us all to forgive and forget about this do you?"

"Name." Stella snapped.

"Okay, okay," he jerked. "Jed Bonner."

"What were you after Jed?"

"If I tell you that, what can you do for me?"

"So now you want to play," she snarled. "George do you feel like playing a game of let's make a deal?"

"It depends," he narrowed his eyes at him. "If he tells us what he was looking for and why."

Jed's hopes soared. He'd lived on the streets most of his life doing a little snatch and grab, pick pocketing, nothing serious and up until now had never been caught. This was big time and bigger since a cop was involved. There was just a chance that he could squeak by on this one.

"Okay, if I tell you what you want, what are you going to do for me?"

"That my young criminal will depend on the information you give us." George wasn't giving in an inch. He knew the boy's type, a street urchin, and knew that he would not get the correct information from him if he showed his hand too soon.

Jed was sweating bullets now. This cop knew his business. He would have to give it up if he hoped this cop would go easy on him.

"I was told there was a certain piece of jewelry here and if I got it I'd get a solid 'G' for it."

"What piece of jewelry?" Stella asked but already knew.

Jed's eyes darted around and then he blinked when they landed on the ring on George's finger. He nodded his head towards it.

"That ring," he said. "That's the ring he said I had to get." He looked confused wondering why he wasn't told the cop was wearing it.

"Who told you to get that ring?" George dashed over to stand next to him, towering over him now. He knew that no one could even touch Geoffrey's ring but Geoffrey and a descendant of his.

What the hell was Geoffrey's game sending an innocent to try and get his ring? It would mean this boy's annihilation should he even touch the ring.

"This guy, I don't know his name," panic took hold of him from the look of steel coming from George's eyes. "Honest I don't know his name. He just said he'd pay me a grand to find it is all."

"Describe him," Stella ordered.

When he did they knew he was talking about Wilfred.

"So do I get a deal?" He looked at them with a sheepish look.

"Oh yes young Jed you get a deal. This will be the deal of a lifetime. You get to stay alive since you never got to touch it and you go into protective custody." George knew the boy's life wasn't worth squat as soon as Wilfred found out he had been made.

George called it in. He was going to direct the officers that come to put young Jed Bonner into a safe house until further notice. He wanted round the clock protection on him.

As they waited for the detail to arrive, they questioned Jed some more.

The only information they got from him was that he was approached by a man with a description that matched Wilfred and that he was promised a 'G' for retrieving the ring. This man approached him on the street and no, he'd never seen him before. Apparently he was told that a P.I. lived in the building and that P.I. was a woman and would be no problem for him.

When an unmarked car pulled up and two men entered the office, George gave them instructions of where to take Jed and to have round the clock protection on him until further notice.

George knew he was going to have to do some fast talking tomorrow to the Chief for this action. He waited until Jed was placed in the car and it drove away.

"George he's just a small time criminal. If Wilfred finds him, we both know that no amount of security on him will stop him." Stella worried for the young misguided criminal and the protective detail assigned to him.

"You and I both know it's the best we can do for him right now," George too worried for him.

"Then let's hope we can catch this Wizard before he finds where you've put that poor kid."

"At least now we know for sure that Geoffrey is behind this and is doing everything he can to locate the ring. Stella that is one thing he can't do." George told her.

"Yeah, but once Wilfred finds out that his little plan didn't work, he'll think of something else and he will look for Jed in order to cover his own ass. Jed Bonner is not safe." Stella told him.

"Stella, all I can do is to keep Jed safe for now. The next move will be up to Wilfred and his father. Let's just hope that somehow we find out what that next move will be before anything happens to Jed Bonner." George shrugged.

CHAPTER

Six

G oing back to bed was out of the question for both of them. Stella went back to the kitchen to fix coffee and breakfast. She had to keep her mind off Wilfred for right now. Thinking of him caused the heat in her to build.

She needed to keep her emotions under control and a clear head. There was no room for mistakes, lives were at stake.

He was getting too close for comfort and hitting them from all angles. She needed time to settle, to reason it all out. Geoffrey was unbound it seemed and he needed his ring if he intended to go up against George. He was getting his son to search for it. There was one ray of hope and that was that Geoffrey knew nothing about her full powers yet. If that is the case, they stood a good chance of defeating him.

The only one who knows where the ring is hidden is George. Maybe that's a good thing, maybe not, her mind worried for him. As she scrambled some eggs George walked into the kitchen and stood in the doorway watching her.

"Stella, you've only caught about an hour's sleep. Our young intruder will be safe for the time being, why don't you go on back to bed?"

"Can't sleep, I need to keep busy right now." She didn't want to turn around and look at him now. She knew her eyes would show him how worried she was about him. He was too good at reading her face.

"Well then I'll help out and make some toast." He walked over to the counter grabbed the loaf of bread and put four slices in the toaster. Pouring two cups of coffee, he took them over to the table sat down and waited for her.

When the bacon and eggs were done she loaded up two plates buttered the toast and carried them to the table to join him.

Not really hungry she shuffled the food around on her plate. After awhile George pushed his aside and took her hand making her look up and into the deep blue pool of his eyes. Her heart did a little flip.

One of ours was responsible for the carnage done to that poor boy, was all she could think about.

"Stella, stop worrying. As long as the ring stays hidden, we have time to find them. He will not dare to try and fight me without it. He is just trying to unbalance us. But as long as we keep our heads he can't even do that."

"I know George. He is hitting us and the people he knows that are close to us. He's either being careful or stupid, now that I think about it, not physically attacking the people we know. If he hurt friends that would certainly unbalance us enough for him to come after us."

"Even unbalanced he is no match against me without his ring." He squeezed her hand, trying to reassure her. "There is one other thing I don't think he is aware of yet and that is the powers you have now. Had he known that, he would never have sent anyone here to look for the ring."

Stella thought about that and it did make sense. If this is true then they have the upper hand. She felt calmer now and suddenly hungry. Stella plowed through her cold breakfast. She sat back patting her full stomach and smiled a wicked smile at him.

"What's going on in that formidable mind of yours?" He raised his eyebrows at her expression.

"Oh I'm just wondering how you are going to explain to Shawn Riley why you took over what should have been a case for his department. He is head of the Burglary Division and I'm sure he is going to hear about this."

George frowned. He had wondered the same thing as soon as he ordered the protective custody on Jed Bonner. "Well I was thinking that since he is your friend, maybe you would be able to smooth the waters there." He gave her an almost irresistible pleading look.

"You're right he is my friend and I am going to keep it that way. You're a smart guy, I'm sure you can figure out a way all by yourself." She knew she was throwing him in at the deep end and laughed.

"And here I thought you loved me."

"With all my heart," she patted his cheek, "but I do not think that you are the kind of man to hide behind a woman's skirts." Now she did laugh long and hard.

'Oh, she would pay for that,' he took a mental note. But he could not help the smile lifting at the corners of his mouth watching the worry fade from her eyes.

The sun slowly crawled through the window making them both realize they had talked through the night. They rinsed off their plates, left them in the sink to dry and headed off to shower, dress and get a start on their respective work.

George left her to have a chat with Shawn. Stella hunkered down at her computer to pick up where she had left off running the financials.

She was only at it for a couple of hours when the phone rang.

"Blake Private Investigator," Stella answered absentmindedly still focusing on her computer.

"Oh my God. Stella, what's wrong? What has happened?" Gwen was frantic on the other end. "When I clued into your mind it gave me such a headache. . ."

"Then keep out of my head, damn it!" Stella yelled at her. "Just because we are sisters does not give you the right to go poking about inside my head whenever you want."

"You're the one that told me to stay on the alert. I figured linking to you will tell me how close Wilfred is getting to us, and trust me linking to your mind is NOT a joy ride for me either." Gwen retaliated.

"Oh and by the way little sister I have not told mother about your conversation with Dr. Ballard." She steamed.

That had Stella's head snapping up. "You know about that?"

"I just told you I was making sporadic links in order to warn the others if I sensed Wilfred getting close. I caught the last part of your conversation with him and Stella, I'm not sure that was a wise move on your part. What if he tells anyone?"

Stella rubbed her face. She wasn't ready to face her family with it right now, she was going to wait and find a way later to let her family know. Now that her sister knows, she would have to tell them. Luck never seemed to be on her side. She had forgotten completely about her sister sneaking peeks into her head.

"Gwen, I trust him." She sighed. "But now I'm having second thoughts about trusting you." Stella seethed at her.

That hit and it hurt for her sister to say that.

Gwen was still seething about it but caught a sense of some of the burden her sister was carrying. She was not jealous of her sister but could not help wondering why she ended up with all the power.

One would think it would go to the one with a calm reasoning rational personality, instead of a kick the door in, spontaneous and charge ahead, damned the consequences personality. But fate had chosen her and they had to believe she knew what she was doing. They had to trust her.

"Stella I know you trust him, but he is after all a human and if that isn't enough, you know Inspector Wise of the RCMP has not closed his file on you. I don't understand why you took this chance."

"Look Gwen, since I accepted our heritage and then found out I was more than other, shall we say, the magic surrounding us has increased and gotten harder and harder to explain. We need someone like Dr. Ballard to be aware so that questions will not be asked."

"He knew something strange was going on," she continued. "He is not only a friend, Gwen, but very good at his job. In fact he is the best and I know it would not be much longer before he started asking awkward questions and would not settle for anything but the truth. He would keep digging."

"Gwen I need you to hold off telling the family for now. They have enough to worry about and with the wedding plans it just is not the right time, okay?" Stella hoped she would listen to reason.

"I haven't told anyone yet. I was waiting until I talked to you about it. I won't say anything until you give me the go, and Stella, I hope you are right about the doctor."

"I am Gwen, I'm sure of it."

"Now tell me about last night." Gwen insisted.

Stella gave her a rundown on the little episode ending up with putting Jed Bonner in protective custody. Then it hit her, she could get Gwen to mind link with him and that would let them know if Wilfred was going after him. If he went after him they would know where to find him and hopefully be there to capture him.

Gwen agreed to do it, she just needed an article from him to link up.

When she hung up, Stella felt like she just dodged a bullet but felt there would be more to come. Revealing their secret could have severe consequences if she was wrong about the good doctor.

After calling George and telling him what she needed for her sister and getting his assurance it would be done, she got back to her work.

She couldn't concentrate. She was tired from lack of sleep. All the numbers were starting to meld together. Stella got up to get a coffee and to clear her mind.

Pacing helped her to focus. The coffee helped to pump up her energy. After a few passes back and forth she stopped. It was time to put up a crime board up and organize all the facts she had so far.

She placed the names of Wilfred and Geoffrey in the center and drew out lines from those. Wilfred to Stanley legal means, Geoffrey to Stanley dead body, Wilfred to Jed my office, looking for the ring.

They were tag teaming. Now was that to keep us running around in circles or to confuse us? 'Circles,' she decided. This way they could direct us to go where they wanted and not have time to go looking for them. 'Very clever,' her eyes narrowed. This way they could separate her and George too, and come after them one at a time. Well she would make damned sure that did not happen.

It settled her knowing she had a bead on what the Wizard and his father were up to. Not that she knew what to do with the discovery, it was good to know that whatever they did next would not surprise her again and have her start chasing her own tail from now on.

Once Jed did not get back to Wilfred about whether or not he found the ring, they will realize we are on to them. Maybe having them chasing their tails searching for him might bring one or both of them out in the open.

Stella's lips curled up in a feral grin. It was time the tables were turned on those to maniacs. Now that she saw more clearly what the pair of them were up to she felt calmer and more in control of the situation.

With her sister keeping an eye on Jed and George back to work in Homicide, she concentrated on her work. With a clear head now, she felt she could relax and wait for the next move Wilfred and his father might come up with.

The one thing she couldn't figure out was how to allow Gwen to participate or even witness the bringing down of those two demented Warlock and Wizard. She knew her sister needed to be in on their capture to gain some of her self confidence back.

It hurt her to see how all this was affecting her sister. Gwen was always the grounded one. She was always sure of herself and accepted the magic that flowed inside her from a very early age.

It was a little humbling to know that she caused so much discord in her own family because of her stubbornness of not relenting on her belief that she was normal and the family was a bit unbalanced, at least in her mind.

Gwen had always accepted her heritage from the very beginning. Stella knew she was a disappointment to her mother and sister by the way she denied what they tried to convince her about this magic blood they professed to all have running through veins.

Now, after accepting the truth, she found that she was stronger in powers than her sister and that had her wonder if Gwen held some resentment towards her for that.

Knowing that she never asked for any of this and ending up being more than her sister weighed heavily on her. Stella determined to sit Gwen down later and talk to her about this. She loves her sister and didn't know if she could bear having Gwen feeling a moment of resentment towards her.

Yes, they teased each other like all siblings do growing up together. Thinking back, she now realized that Gwen only goaded her to try to get her onboard with what truly flowed through their veins. But Gwen didn't realize that she also suffered the teasing of other children along with her sister's flare for inciting her anger. She felt she could not go to her mother or sister about all the drama and trauma she suffered at the hands of the other schoolmates. Only Maria was privy to her troubles at the time and through those young years was there to support her and show her love and consideration throughout those years.

Being attacked on two levels had Stella hiding within herself, keeping more and more feelings buried inside. She felt she had no support and was forced to handle everything on her own. This only made her suspicious of everyone she came into contact with while growing up. Gwen and her mother never knew how she felt or what she was going through at that time. At that time Stella felt neither of them would understand or even wish to help her. It was only Maria that knew what she was going through at that time.

She not only had to deal with the teasing and taunting at school but the disappointed and disgusted attitude from her mother and sister because she could not force herself to believe what they tried to force upon her.

At that time Maria was the only one she felt she could go to for comfort and understanding. Not knowing that Maria was a Witch at that time, she felt she was the only one that she could lean on and tell her about how she felt at that time.

Now it was up to her to save her family and find a way for Gwen to feel a part of taking down a Wizard and his Warlock father that tried to kill her.

Now that she has finally faced the fact that she is filled with magic and that magic is stronger than her mother's and her sister's, Stella was now faced with keeping them all safe. She knew deep down that she needs to rely on her logical thinking as well as the magic flowing in her blood to do this. Proving she is more than either one is going to be a hurdle for her sister, who believed from the very beginning. Stella had to wonder why this power did not go to her older sister instead of her. Gwen was calmer and believed from the start. This power should have been hers. She wondered, and not for the first time, why she was chosen to have it and not Gwen.

Then Stella wondered how she would feel if her older sister did have this power instead of her, how she would feel about that. That thought had her wonder how Gwen would deal with the situations she's been forced to deal with. It struck her then that Gwen would want to take time to rationalize and waste time doing that and put them all in jeopardy. Gwen was not one to be physical but diplomatic and that cannot work when dealing with Warlocks. Instinctively Stella knew that Gwen would not be able to stand over a body destroyed by a Warlock and keep her thinking rational. She's had no training in homicide.

A Warlock killing was more gruesome than any other homicide. What they do to a human body is not something most people can deal with. Gwen was too gentle and would never get over it. A sight like that would haunt her for the rest of her life.

Thinking of this helped Stella to realize why she is the chosen one. Standing over many dead people in her chosen career as the Lieutenant of Homicide has prepared her for this. Also seeing and speaking to spirits, although that is one part of her gift she has never liked, but it has her more prepared for this power she's been given.

For once she is very thankful that her sister never has to deal with those things. Gwen could never cope with this part of the gifts she's been given. Her heart is way too soft and caring and giving. Instinctively Stella knew this part would destroy her sister.

This is such a revelation to her. Just to know now that Gwen could not cope with this situation, never dawned on her before. Gwen was always the more logical and rational of the two of them. She was the one that accepted what flowed in them. Stella never believed the stories they tried to convince her of. Now that she found out that she is more gifted than her sister didn't sit well with her. It was like she has become more than her sister and mother, that fact she is having a big problem with.

CHAPTER

Seven

She spent the rest of the day finishing up on the financials on Pete's employees and came up empty. That should be a big relief for him knowing that none of them betrayed him and he could still trust them. Stella decided that she would need to head her investigation toward others in his administrative section. Since none of the workers in the plant knew about the new engine plans, it had to be someone in management. Checking her watch she saw she didn't have enough time to reach Mr. Yamada before he left for the day.

The best she could do was to make an appointment to see him tomorrow and get the files on his managerial staff before shutting down for the day. Stretching to relieve some of the tension that built up from her time on the computer, she locked up and went into her own quarters.

Rifling through her cupboards trying to come up with an idea for supper, she settled on heating up a can of soup. Her mind just would not close down enough to put a meal together.

George walked in as she sat eating her soup. She looked up and saw the tired lines on his face. She got up to go fill a bowl for him stroking his cheek softly on her way by.

They sat in silence eating. Both busy with their own thoughts. When they finished and rinsed out their bowls, they went to relax in the living room. George poured them both a glass of wine and settled onto the sofa beside her. They both leaned back resting their feet on the scarred coffee table.

George curled a lank of her hair around his finger peering at her over the rim of his glass.

"It seems we have both had a long day." He said softly.

"Yeah," she breathed out. "I think I might have an angle with the Yamada case. I'll know better tomorrow when I get the files from him and go over them."

"How was your day?" She was putting off telling him what she puzzled together about Wilfred and his father. She knew he had to talk to Shawn about the burglary and taking the suspect into protective custody.

'Oh to be a fly on that wall,' she chuckled to herself.

Looking at her, George quirked an eyebrow up as he guessed her thoughts. But he instinctively knew she was also holding something back from him. He decided to play along knowing she would tell him when she was ready.

"It started off digging my way out from under a mountain of paperwork and ending with a chat with Shawn." He paused.

"Yes, well, at first he was not too pleased with me, but I finally managed to get him to come around to my way of thinking."

"What did it cost you?" She knew Shawn better than he did.

"You are right, it did cost me," now he chuckled. "Did you know he was a huge fan of the Blue Jays?"

"Yup, we used to go to the opening game together every year."

"Well he is now the proud owner of the best seat for all the home games this year." Now he did laugh shaking his head. "He drives a very hard bargain."

"He makes me so proud," she pretended to wipe away an imaginary tear.

"You would think that wouldn't you?" he smiled down at her. "Now how about you tell me what you haven't told me. What's been going on in that delightful brain of yours?"

Oh he was good at reading her.

Damn, she thought, he always knows when I'm holding something from him. Does he have some secret radar system? It didn't matter that she was going to tell him, it was just that he always knows when I have something and don't share it with him straight away. Stella wriggled uncomfortably beside him.

"It's nothing really. It's just that I see things clearer when I can actually see them lined up. I decided to make a crime board and put down all the facts we know so far."

"And what precisely did that clear up for you?"

Stella went through the steps of putting all the facts on the board and told him the picture she drew from it.

"So you figure we have been led around by the nose by those two." Seeing it in his mind the way she described, he could see the logic in it.

"That's the way it ended up looking to me." She stared into her glass frowning. "Unless you see something different," she added.

"No, it makes sense Stella. Geoffrey is prone to be theatrical as we have experienced from the last encounter with him. I would say you hit the mark right on. And I think you are right about them going around searching for Jed."

"Yeah, your detectives will not be able to protect him if they find out where you have him hidden." She paused and looked up at him with worry in her eyes. "You know they will kill your men George."

He knew what she was thinking and rejected it.

"I will not ask your mother to take him in. That will put a thief in her house and danger at her door. No," he shook his head determined to have his way.

"Where else would he be safe? They can't reach him there."

"We'll have to come up with something else, Stella. I will not bring that trouble to your mother. I am firm on this."

She could tell there was no budging him on this point. She sighed.

"Okay, George," she gave in. "I've got Gwen linking with him now that she has something of his. I hope that will be enough warning for us."

"I will go over there tomorrow and put up a bit of a warning signal in case Gwen misses any clues to any danger. I will also put up a shield to keep them busy enough until I can get there. We just have to hope that will be enough and I can get there in time."

"George I know Jed's a criminal, but he is also an innocent."

"Then we had better find them before they can get to him."

There was no way she would get him to change his mind. As frustrating as it was, she had to give way to his terms. Battling with him would only hurt their relationship and deep down she was grateful that her mother would not be put in direct danger by having the lad there.

She let it go. Secretly she did wish that he would go there now and set up his special alarm system. But he felt that he had time and it can wait until tomorrow.

The next morning Stella met with Mr. Yamada. Although he kept a pretty good poker face, she detected a sign of relief that none of his engineers betrayed him.

As she requested he handed over all the files on his administrative personnel. She was on her way out when a thought struck her. Stella walked over to his personal secretary's desk.

"Gloria," she glanced down at the young woman sitting behind her desk.

"Yes Miss Blake?" She looked up, a tiny frown on her face seeing the personnel files in Stella's hand.

"I know what I have to do is uncomfortable for you. But I was just wondering if there had been any temps working here over the last few months."

"One moment please," Gloria tapped a few keys on her keyboard bringing up a new screen on her computer.

"Yes, we had two temporaries within the last two months. One worked in purchasing while Mr. Prescott's secretary was off sick and the other was here for two weeks while I was on my honeymoon."

Tingle.

"Gloria do you have access to any papers submitted in from the engineering department?" Stella kept her face blank.

"Of course I do. When they send in their reports or requests for changes, Mr. Yamada goes over them and has me type up any changes he wishes to make. I can assure you Miss Blake that everything that comes before me is held in the strictest confidence." She puffed up at the insinuation that she would leak any information.

"Do you keep copies of all the reports?"

"Well of course I do. They remain here locked up in this office."

"Thank you Gloria that's good to know. I wonder if you would be good enough to give me the files of the two temps please."

"Miss Blake we screen our temporary helpers very thoroughly."

"I am sure that you do. The files please," Stella insisted.

Gloria stood up shoving her chair back furious that this woman could think for one minute that someone in the administrative staff could possibly be guilty of leaking confidential information. She pulled the files out of the cabinet and handed them to her, almost tossing them at her.

Stella thanked her and left the red faced private secretary silently fuming.

As she drove back to her office, Stella felt sure she would find the answers to Mr. Yamada's problem inside one of the files that rested on the seat beside her.

As she turned onto Main Street, the hairs on the back of her neck stood up. She shivered. Frantically looking in her mirrors for the cause, she found nothing alarming, nothing out of the ordinary. If someone was tailing her, he was very good as she could not spot it. Traffic was light and not many people walking about. No one stood out to her. The sensation lasted until she pulled up in her driveway.

Stella climbed out of her car and glanced around. Mrs. Witcomb, her neighbour stopped shaking the dust out of a throw rug to wave at her. Stella sent up an involuntary wave as she continued up her walk. There was no one else around. She shook her head as she walked into her office.

Sitting behind her desk she still could not shake the feeling of being watched. It was a strange feeling. No one was in the office but her, yet she felt eyes on her. She pulled out her phone and called George.

"Hi darling, I'm just on my way to the morning squad meeting."

The way he said 'darling' made her face grow hot. It seemed amazing to her how he had the ability to melt her bones at a single word or look.

Stella cleared her throat to cover the emotions running through her.

"Sorry, this won't take long. I just wondered if you did the little job we talked about last night."

He smiled hearing the huskiness in her voice. He had to bank his own lust from the images the tone of her voice put into his head.

"I did yes. Don't worry Stella. We should have enough time should there be a need."

"One more thing, um,,," she hesitated to tell him of the unsettling feeling she felt.

"What is it? What's wrong Stella?" Her hesitation sent internal alarm bells ringing.

"Maybe nothing, I just wondered if you have heard anything about the RCMP, and, you know, me."

"Stella, you and I both know Inspector Wise is still interested in you, but I don't think he would chance another illegal tailing or bugging. I've got a friend in that bureau and he promised to let me know if they were coming after you again. I have not heard anything yet.

"What has happened for you to think so?" Stella's instincts were always right. If she was worried about this there had to be a reason for it.

"I am being watched but I can't pin point where it's coming from."

"I will check in with my friend. Meanwhile watch your step and be careful."

'Yeah like she needed to be told that,' she thought as she hung up.

Her skin still pricked at the feeling of being watched. She decided to keep herself busy going through the files she took from Mr. Yamada's office.

After a short time the feeling of being watched stopped. Stella breathed in a huge sigh of relief. But in the back of her mind, she held onto that feeling. If it was the RCMP, they would get a surprise should they try to surprise her with a visit.

But something told her this was not the RCMP, but something else. She did wonder if Geoffrey or his son had found a way to watch her without revealing themselves.

George had refused to tell Stella where they were holding Jed Bonner. So whoever was watching her would not get that information from her. She wondered if that was what was at play. She wondered if they had a way to actually watch her hoping that she would lead them to him or even if they could read her mind.

Stella called George to ask him if his talents leaned in that direction. When he told her that no, Warlocks could not read minds like her sister, she felt a bit calmer.

For Stella to ask that question, told him she was more worried than she let on. Now George worried about the sensation she was feeling. Knowing that his line did not possess that power, he began to wonder if there wasn't someone or something else in play.

George spent his time at work dividing his mind between work and worry over her. If someone was watching her, and it was not a Warlock or Wizard, he feared that something else had come to add to their problems.

Now the problem was to try to remember the powers from the Warlock World. He remembered stories of Seers and imps, and of course Witches stemmed from that World as well. There were others but he couldn't bring them to mind at the moment.

Other than Witches, Warlocks and Wizards, he knew very little about the gifts of Seers and Imps. Maybe there were a few of them sprinkled down through the lineage and living in the Human World. It might be possible that they could watch without detection. This left him feeling a little nervous.

George felt that he should check through his archives to find if they contain any mention of other magic in the Warlock World. Up until the time he met up with Stella he'd only encountered Warlocks, Wizards, Witches and Imps. Now he figures he should check into his ancestral background to see if there are others, beside Seers. If memory served him right, Seers didn't have much power other than looking into a scrying bowl to reach out to keep their eye on what is happening in their World. This gave him some hope to come up with some answers he didn't have before. Maybe in his archives he will find the answer to who is watching Stella and making her nervous.

CHAPTER
Eight

Stella had a chance to speak to most of the employees in management and got a sense of total loyalty. No one in his administrative staff had anything but the highest respect for their boss. She decided to go through all their files first to eliminate them once and for all. In her gut she knew it had to be one of the temps that worked there. This again was her gift pointing her in the right direction.

It took hours to go through them. She had just finished with his full time people and about to run the temp in purchasing when the door to her office opened.

Since she stayed on full alert over the uncomfortable feeling that refused to go away, she had her gun out in a flash and pointed at the person walking into her office.

Louise let out a scream at the sight of the gun aimed at her. She stood frozen with fear, her hands clutched at her heart. Her eyes went so wide they seemed to swallow her face.

Feeling foolish for having acted on pure adrenalin, she lowered the gun and slowly placed it back in its holster. Shaking her head, she got up and went over to the terrified Louise.

"I'm so sorry Louise," she said rubbing Louise's arms.

"M . . . my fault," Louise stuttered through chattering teeth. "I . . . I should have knocked." She let Stella steer her over to a chair and collapsed into it.

"No, Louise, it was my fault. I should not have reacted like that." Stella poured Louise a coffee and handed it to her.

"Thanks," Louise took it in shaky hands. After a few sips, colour returned to her face and the shaking stopped.

"I forgot how dangerous your work can be Stella. I'm really glad we're friends and not enemies." Louise tried a weak laugh. "You scared ten years off my life."

"I'm really sorry Louise. I'm a little edgy right now." She wanted to offer some kind of excuse.

"A little edgy," Louise squeaked. "I would hate to see what you would do if you were a lot edgy." She couldn't help the shudder.

Stella ignored that, glad to see she had her spunk back. She left her to go sit behind her desk.

"Now that the fun and games are over," she cocked her head to the side, "what brings you here?"

"Fun and games she calls it," Louise snorted. "I have been sent as a messenger from Deb. She needs you to set some time aside for a fitting for your wedding dress."

True fear ran straight through her at the very idea of wearing something her friend designed. Oh, she was the top fashion designer, but Deb's designs were not suited to her. She was not the feather, sequin or filmy flamboyant type. She was more the elegant subtle demure but chic type. Dior and Versace was more her style. Once in awhile Chanel came up with designs that did please her. Vera Wang was way too modern for her taste.

Louise couldn't help it. The look of utter terror on Stella's face had her peeling in laughter.

"Oh sure you can laugh Louise, you are not picturing yourself looking like an ostrich." Stella barked. "I think I might just order something through a catalogue."

That stopped the laughter dead. "Oh no, you will not. You will not hurt that delightful girl that way. She is your best friend. Deb is so happy to do this for you. If you do not let her do this, you will crush her. She loves you." Louise jumped out of her chair leaned over planting both hands on the desk, going almost nose to nose with Stella. Her face bloomed red as a beet with anger. "You will call her and make an appointment for the fitting."

Oh crap.

Stella leaned back in her chair to get Louise's face out of hers. Louise didn't need a gun to terrorize her, her temper was enough, and she knew she was right. It would really hurt Deb if she didn't let her do this. "I'll just cancel the photographer," Stella figured at least she wouldn't be humiliated by photos of her unorthodox and probably cartoonish wedding gown. 'But oh my God,' she thought, 'what was she going to look like on her wedding day?'

Stella put her hands up in defeat. "Okay, okay I'll set it up. Now cool the thrusters Louise." Stella frowned. "Did George ever win any arguments with you?"

"No," Louise brushed her hands over her suit, satisfied, she sat back down again. "And you will not cancel the photographer," Louise adamantly told her.

"I can understand why not. You really are formidable and you don't even need a gun."

Louise laughed. "We each have our own brand of weapon."

"I got to say, yours is deadly and your aim is right on target." Now they both laughed. Secretly she was holding on to the thought of canceling the photographer.

"Stella is it safe for me to be here? You did pull your gun out. Are you expecting some kind of danger?" Louise sent her a worried look.

"I'm sorry for that Louise. No you are not in danger here. It was just a reflex action." Stella tried to brush it off.

Louise wasn't convinced but she let it go, for now. She knew if it had something to do with a case she was working on, Stella would not divulge any information. She just hoped that whatever was putting that strained look on her face would be solved soon.

Louise left with Stella promising to contact Deb for a dress fitting appointment.

Stella went back to doing the background checks. The girl in purchasing checked out. There was nothing in her financials, family or friends to suspect her.

She started on the temp for Gloria. It didn't take long for a connection to be found. Elaine Farmer was engaged to Robert White, an engineer for Ford's.

Tingle.

Her financials didn't show anything suspicious, but her connection with another engine company did.

Stella wrote down all her information and decided to pay Elaine a visit the next day. Stella shut down her computer, called Deb and arranged a time for her to do her thing, then locked up the office before heading back to her quarters.

Just talking to Deb about her dress had her stomach queasy. She needed to do something to get her mind off it. She decided to take a shower before George arrived.

She was just tying her hair back when she heard him come in the back door. She finished dressing slipping into an old pair of jeans and a Blue Jay t-shirt before going out to meet him. She found him in the living room pouring two glasses of wine. He turned when he heard her step into the room. Holding out one of the glasses for her, she walked over took it and rose up on her toes to press her lips to his. The taste of her lips would leave any wine paling in comparison.

"Hello," she whispered against his lips before turning with her wine to take a seat on the sofa.

"Hello," his voice betrayed his needs.

"Come and sit down," she patted the cushion beside her.

"I will, but first I want to get out of this suit." And get his glands under control, he thought.

Stella took a sip of wine while fluttering her lashes at him. It felt so good to let go of the day's problems. It made her feel giddy and girlish.

It did take him a bit longer than normal to change clothes. George walked back into the living room. Watching her behave strangely puzzled him for a moment.

For some reason it did not surprise her to realize he had the power to bring out the deeply buried feminine side of her. She had never flirted with any man before him. Her life had always been filled with education and work. She only dated a few times to scratch an itch.

Once the itch was taken care of and went away she sent the man away too. She always made sure it was only a mutual thing and not a romantic entanglement. Watching his reaction was giving her a high, filling her with a heady flavour of ambrosia.

George raised his eyebrows at her. This was so out of character for her. He felt himself the master of the art of flirtation, but never dreamt that Stella had it in her. Although it gave him a wonderful sensation to see her expertly using her wiles, it just wasn't his Stella.

Something was off.

He left the room to change his clothes and took a bit longer than needed to try to figure out why she was acting this way. When he walked back into the living room he found her lazing on the sofa in a very provocative way. Of course lust bloomed in his loins, it always did when he looked at her, but something was off, way off and he banked his lust until he could figure out the reason for why she was acting this way.

"Come here darling," Stella crooked a finger at him beckoning him over to her.

"Stella, what is going on?" he walked over to her but remained standing.

"Why should anything be wrong just because I want to make love to you?" Her face glowed smiling up at him.

And then a thought suddenly occurred to her. Wouldn't it be fun to see if she could get George to reveal a secret to her? She'd find out just how much he loved her. After all, lovers should never hide secrets from each other. She began to giggle as she stared up at him.

And there it was, a hint of something black behind her eyes. He took two steps back. Waving his hand he chanted sending up a shield around them both. The strange thing behind her eyes vanished. Stella sat up and shook her head. She felt dizzy and sick. George seeing this rushed over to her and pushed her head down between her knees.

She breathed in and out slowly until the dizziness faded. Raising her head, she looked up into his eyes, confused.

"I'm sorry, I don't know what's wrong with me." She rubbed her hands over her face finding it clammy.

"Now there's the Stella I know and love." George felt relieved to see her back to normal.

"What?"

"You were not yourself Stella. You were being controlled." Flames shot out of him from rage.

"What? Controlled? How? Who? That can't be."

"You will be glad to know you were right Stella. You were being watched, but not from the outside. From inside. Somehow they were able to get inside you."

"How?" Instantly she was alert and very angry.

"It's a very old charm, so old I had almost forgotten about it. It's a very good thing you have no knowledge of the ring's whereabouts or they would have had it by now."

His words hit her hard. They had controlled her from inside her without her knowledge. Fear swept in her to mix with the anger bubbling up wanting to spill over. She battled to keep calm knowing rage would only cloud the mind. It appeared they had more tricks up their sleeves than she knew about. She knew something had to be done so this could never happen again.

"First we were wrong. They didn't go after Jed like we thought they would, they came after one of us. Second and most important, how do I stop them from putting that charm on me again?"

"It has been centuries since that charm was used on a Fairy, I will have to look into my archives for the protective charm." If he had to, he would keep his shield up all night until he could get to the archives.

"You said it was used on a Fairy."

"Yes, I remember reading something about that in my collection."

"Would Ravena know how to thwart that charm then?"

"I would not imagine so, but Gareg would, I should think."

"Okay, give me some room," She got up off the sofa as George stepped away from her.

Stella lifted her arms and called on the heat to build. As it built the wind swirled around her lifting her in the air, loosening her hair to fly around her face. Her green eyes sent sparks shooting from them. She slowly began to rotate and called upon her Queen.

"Ravena Queen of the Fairy World, I call upon you to come before me and witness what we do."

A golden oval appeared encrusted with jewels that shot out a rainbow of light from them. In the center Ravena appeared in her regal gown and crown.

"My child it is always a pleasure to see you. Are you well?"

"Yes my Queen I am well."

"You look troubled my child. How can I help you?"

Stella told Ravena of the charm that was put on her and that George thought Prince Gareg would know the protective charm. Ravena listened quietly and nodded her head after hearing her out. Her image left the oval to fetch the Prince.

When Gareg appeared, George bowed to him and Stella let George take over the conversation.

"My Prince," George bowed again.

"My son, it is a pleasure to see you again. Now pray tell me the trouble."

"Yes your Highness," George explained what had happened and that he is positive about the kind of charm that was put on Stella.

"I am familiar with this charm. We had a similar problem here. There is another charm to combat that one." Prince Gareg told George the charm and wished him well.

They both wished the royal couple a heartfelt goodbye and watched the oval ring disappear. Stella released the heat and slowly floated back to the floor. When the wind died away George was there to catch her before she fell limply to the floor. That was one side affect she hated, the way transforming lately drained her of her strength. It must have something to do with the speed in which she was changing and growing in her new powers.

He sat her gently on the sofa, and then took a few steps back to perform the charm Gareg gave him.

Once the charm was completed he sat down beside her, took her face in his hands and gently kissed her lips, and pulling her close to him, murmured in her ear.

"As much as I enjoyed that little seduction act, it just was not my Stella. I love the Stella you really are."

"Hmm, didn't know I had the femme fatal in me. Glad to know," she wiggled her eyebrows at him. Then her eyes narrowed. "I am going to kick his ass for this when we find him."

"Now that is definitely the Stella I know and love," George laughed happy beyond words that she was back.

"Well you better, because I am no one's girly girl." Stella growled. "And no one's puppet either."

George kissed her soundly then he pulled back a bit from her to perform another chant. This one released the shield around them. He watched her closely to see if Gareg's spell worked.

Looking deep into her eyes, he saw that they remained clear. The spell worked and he breathed a sigh of relief. Now he pulled her into his arms and kissed her with deep passion.

Stella reciprocated his embrace with one of her own. Lust bloomed in them both from what they gave to each other.

"Oh Stella, I don't know what I'd do without you. I never want to lose you. No matter what the two of them throw at us, I'll never stop loving you," George sighed holding her tight.

"Well as interesting as that was, I never ever want to feel like that again. I'm sorry George, but I'm just not the femme fatale those two wanted me to be." She shuddered at the thought. "I am a kick-ass in your face person and always have been. Now I want to kill them." Her eyes narrowed.

"Then I'm happy to say that I agree with you. Had you been a femme fatale, I'd never have been drawn to you. I happen to love the kick-ass part of you. Trophy women and models never could hold my attention." He assured her.

"Oh George, that is just not me. I hate it when my feelings are tampered with. I'm a kick-ass woman. I was Lieutenant in my squad and could do my job. This, whatever he did to me was just not me. I want to really hurt him more than you can imagine." She seethed.

"I hope you know that I want them just as badly as you do," George told her.

"There is no way he is going to touch any of my family George. I vow to you right now that I will do whatever it takes to stop him and his demented son." Stella's eyes filled with rage.

It felt so good for them both to be back to who they really are. Theirs is a love like no other. The bond between them is like no other. They were indelibly linked in mind heart and soul. To lose one would lose them both. Something deep inside them told them this. The only love they can compare to what they have is the love between Queen Ravena and her Prince Gareg. No Human, no matter how much they love, can ever come close to what they have.

CHAPTER
Nine

E ven though neither one mentioned it, they both knew what the seduction was all about. It was Geoffrey trying to get Stella to trick George into revealing to her the location of the ring.

Tired from a long day and calling up the Queen, Stella turned in wanting to shut her brain off and give it a rest. She knew George performed the charm spell correctly but the uneasy feeling of being watched still hung around. She worried that maybe Geoffrey had found a way around the spell, but then she didn't feel different from herself like she did earlier.

It was the feeling of her mind being violated that she couldn't shake. Now she knew exactly how her sister felt when she walked into her office to find someone had touched her things and strewn her possessions all around.

That thought had her falling asleep thinking of checking out her place and car for hidden cameras and bugs. Just in case the RCMP were up to their old tricks again.

Stella woke up groggy the next morning. Putting on her shabby old housecoat and floppy slippers she shuffled to the kitchen in search of coffee and George, in that order. A fresh pot was brewing on the counter but no George. She poured a cup and took it to the table where she found a note addressed to her.

> Good morning my love. You were so tired from last night I did not want to wake you. There is a pot of fresh coffee brewing. I'll talk to you later.
>
> You are my heart.....George

How can you be angry with someone who can think to write something like that? To be so considerate, her heart melted into goo. Then she happened to catch a glimpse of the clock over the stove and yelped. "Nine o'clock," she'd never slept in so late.

"What the hell was he thinking? Half my morning is gone and I've got work to do. Oh, he is going to hear from me." She stomped in her floppy slippers to the shower.

She was showered and dressed in half the normal time it took her. Riding on a fury she gathered up what she needed and put in a test call to Elaine's apartment. Getting no answer, she assumed Elaine was at a new temping job.

Perfect.

She drove over to the address listed in her file and parked across the street from the apartment building. 'Well now,' she thought, 'A person would think Sunset Towers is a bit pricey for a temp's salary.' Since it boasted a doorman it must also have good security as well. Stella decided to sit, wait and watch before making her move.

While she waited, Stella took out her camera and snapped shots of people going in and out. The doorman seemed to be very familiar with everyone.

It was closing in on noon when she caught her chance to get inside. The doorman was a smoker, bless his heart. She watched him check around before heading off to grab a smoke around the corner of the building.

It was lucky for her that she had misplaced her master key when she was on the force and was given another to replace it. And lucky again that she found the missing master key months later and decided to hold on to it. It wouldn't do for her to be seen picking the lock on the outer door to the building.

Stella jumped out of the car crossed the street in a flash and fit the key inside the lock. The red light turned green and she was in. There was nothing she could do about the security cameras in the lobby. All she could do was try to keep her face away from them.

Stella kept her head down making her way to the elevator. As soon as the doors opened she quickly stepped in. From the address she was given, Elaine lived on the fourth floor. She pushed the button for four and waited for the doors to close.

On the short ride up she had time to get out her lock picks and had them ready when the doors slowly opened onto her floor. She walked down the carpeted hallway and stopped at the last door on the right. After a quick glance over her shoulder to make sure she was unobserved, she knelt down and worked the picks in the lock. It only took a couple of seconds for her to unlock the door.

Stella put her tools away and slid silently into Elaine's apartment. Her first thought was that someone had got there before her and ransacked the place. But on closer inspection she realized the chaos was done by Elaine.

Discarded clothes were carelessly tossed over chairs and laying on the floor. The furniture looked like it had not been cleaned or dusted in days. Winding her way through the mess she noticed the kitchen sported dirty dishes on the table, counter and sink. 'My God, she thought. 'This girl is a complete slob.'

Seeing no need to be careful about going through her things since it wouldn't be noticed in any case, she began searching every room. It was a two bedroom apartment and one of the bedrooms was set up for a personal office. Stella headed straight for the file cabinet and hit pay dirt. Among the files were copies of Yamada Engine's new design along with copies made from a few other companies of their blueprints and confidential papers. There goes the theory that Elaine was an innocent duped by her lover. This clearly shows that she is a fully fledged partner in crime with her boyfriend.

Stella took pictures of all the paperwork before putting them back in the cabinet. She knew she could not go to the police with the evidence without being charged with B&E herself. Now that she knew Elaine was guilty she would have to catch her red handed.

She locked up went down and was climbing in her car when the doorman walked back around the corner of the building to stand at his post again. Before starting her car, Stella put a call into her friend at the revenue service to locate where Elaine was now employed.

Just as she pulled into her driveway, she felt the uncomfortable feeling of being watched again. Remembering her last thoughts before drifting off last night, she got busy first checking her car and then going around in her office and private quarters checking for hidden cameras and bugs. She found nothing and that made her even edgier wondering if somehow Geoffrey found a way to watch her from a distance.

Her sister had the gift of reading a person's mind, not watching from without. Her mother could only see a person in some sort of distress to describe in vague terms the area that person is in. This felt more like eyes on her watching her but not knowing what is in her mind or how she is feeling.

Stella decided it was time to go into self protection mode and placed a shield around her building. Once she completed that, the feeling went away. And because it did go away she knew it had nothing to do with the RCMP or any human surveillance. Whoever was watching her was from the magic world.

She called George.

"Homicide Lieutenant Smale." His voice rang out clear.

"George are you alone?"

He heard the concern in her voice. "Not at the moment but I can be. What's wrong?" His whole body stiffened at her tone. He was on full alert.

"No George, don't do anything out of the ordinary. When you get a moment to yourself, call me back." She hung up.

George looked at the phone listening to the dial tone before hanging it up. He looked up at the officer he had been dressing down before the phone rang. With part of his mind on Stella, he finished with the officer who was quaking in his shoes after this particular tongue lashing. Seeing the effect this disciplinary action had on the young officer, George knew he'd be very sure of never making the same mistake twice. As soon as he dismissed him he got up closed and locked the door, then quickly called her back.

"Okay Stella I'm alone. What's wrong? I can be there in ten minutes."

She was powerful and he knew she could take care of herself, but she called him. He was starting to panic that she might have come up against something she could not handle on her own.

"No, no George I don't need you here right now. Sorry to worry you. It's just that I have had the feeling of being watched and now I know it's not human, so it's not the RCMP. I need to ask you something."

"First tell me are you in any danger?" Everything in him wanted to hang up and rush over to her, but he stayed on the phone with her.

"I don't think so. But I need to know if you have the gift of watching someone from a distance. Can you watch without being in the same vicinity?"

"No Stella, I have to be in the same area to sense another. I can only sense someone, not actually see that person. Why?"

"Well the feeling I get is eyes on me. I can't explain it any other way. It's like someone has a set of binoculars on me no matter where I go."

"I'll be there in ten minutes." George hung up determined not to listen to her refusing his help.

Stella hung up the phone and sighed. If he could not do what was happening to her he could be in danger just being near her. There was nothing she could do now but wait and hope nothing would happen to him.

Less than ten minutes later, she heard him yelling for her outside her office. The protective shield she put around her building was keeping him out.

Stella stepped out took his hand and walked him through the shield with her. She saw the panic look fade when he saw her step out of the building. It was replaced by a look of awe when she led him into the building.

"My God Stella, I've never come up against a shield that powerful before. Maybe I should take you over to the safe house and you can put that up around it."

"No because you cannot tell me where the safe house is until I find out who is watching me. Do you think Geoffrey has the power to see me from somewhere else?"

"I would have to say no. I think his powers are the same as mine and without his ring his powers are very limited and weaker now."

"I was afraid you were going to say that. That means there is a new player in town and a powerful one." Stella began pacing back and forth.

"If there is and if he's working with Geoffrey we have a serious problem." George frowned. He never envisioned another Warlock with more powers than himself. This one it seems might be a threat even to Stella.

"George I can't risk anything happening to my family. I don't know if I can protect them." Tears stung behind her eyes.

George went to her and folded her in his arms. She was visibly shaken with this new development.

Her office phone rang the same time her cell phone did. Torn between the two, the look on her face was comical but neither of them felt the humour at the moment. George took the initiative and went over to answer the office phone leaving her to deal with the caller on her cell.

"Stella, Stella, oh my God Stella," Stella had to hold the phone away from her ear from her sister screaming in it. "Who can it be? What can we do? How are we to survive?"

"Gwen stop your yelling. This is exactly what you get for invading my privacy."

"Oh fuck that! You know perfectly well why I'm linked to you. You knew I would know exactly what is happening. We need to get the family together and leave here and find somewhere safe."

Stupid, stupid, stupid, she had forgotten all about her sister linking with her until she just reminded her. How could she have been so stupid? She should have remembered and blocked her somehow.

Too late now.

"Gwen we don't know for sure what this person wants. Whoever it is might not be working with Geoffrey. Until we know for sure we can do nothing. But I think the family should be told about it. We can only hope that the Manor is protected against this person."

"Then I'll call mom and get her to gather everyone there now." Gwen's voice was shaky.

"Yes, alright you call mom and get things set up there. George and I still have some work to do and we will join you all later."

"Stella, this is more important than your damned work. You need to go to the Manor now." Having a plan gave her back some of her courage.

Stella was glad to hear the sound of a bossy big sister rather than the terrified woman. But knowing an hour or two here or there was not going to make any difference, she would finish whatever work needed doing on her case before she went to meet the family.

Okay, she was just a little bit of a coward and wanted some time before she had to deal with the drama scene at her mother's.

When she ended her call and slipped her phone back into her pocket, George walked over handing her a piece of paper with the message from her friend at the revenue service. She took the paper and read the name of Elaine's new employer. Seeing the name of the Toyota plant on it had her shaking her head at Elaine's predictability, and the incredible obtuseness of all her employers not tracking the criminal act back to her.

"Stella, I think Gwen is right. We should go to your mother's and tell them all about this. It might be a good idea for you to put your own shield around the Manor for their protection as well."

"George, remember you could not enter without mom's permission. If this is a Warlock he is under the same rules. They should be fine until we go over later on." She stroked his cheek seeing the worried look on his face.

His hand went up to hold hers' against his face. "Stella, I have never known another Warlock to have different powers. Different strengths of powers, yes, but to have extra powers beyond what we all possess, I have never come across that before." He was clearly worried for her now.

"Do you think you should tell the Queen?"

Something fluttered inside her. Somehow she knew telling her that the Queen was not the answer.

"No, at least not for now, not yet George. I can't explain it but I think we need to find out more before I do that."

George knew no amount of pushing was going to change her mind. He had to believe she knew what she was doing. All he could do now was to support her decision and stay close to her in case this person decided watching her was not enough and tried to act against her.

Inside it shocked him to see her standing so strong. Here was something neither one has ever dealt with and her confidence is up and her thinking was clear.

George knew it was he that was starting to panic and knew he had to come to terms quickly about the change in her. He knew he had to go from protector to partner with her and that was becoming an uphill battle. But this battle had to be won; he had to allow her to be whomever and whatever she is now.

The growth in her was both startling and amazing to watch. He felt so proud of her, but at the same time he couldn't help worrying about her too. She was no longer just a necromancer, but so much more and it is all new to her.

He marveled at all the changes going on in her and that her confidence was also growing inside of her.

This was a new Stella, but inside he knew she was still the Stella that he fell in love with. Something inside him told him that he had to come to terms with this and accept what she was becoming. Nothing mattered as long as they remained together and loved each other.

That had him stepping back just a little to give her the room to grow and be who she was always meant to be. His love for her would never diminish because of this new revelation. His ego was another thing. Something told him his ego was about to be challenged to the max and he sincerely hopes he can handle that. His ego could cause a shift or break in their relationship and that must never happen.

Listening to her give clear concise decisions filled him with such great pride he felt almost bursting with it. Not that long ago she coward in his arms at all the magic that came her way. Now she stands tall and ready to face the magic with confidence. It was like watching a caterpillar transform into a beautiful butterfly.

He couldn't help but marvel at the changes she's gone through. This kick-ass woman, not that long ago, who was ready to collapse with all the incredible incidences that came to her causing her world to shatter and fall all around her, now stood strong and decisive. She simply undid him.

As strong as his foster sister always showed she was, she could not come close to the strength Stella was now showing. George felt humbled in Stella's presence.

CHAPTER

Ten

E ven though he had a battle going on inside, George met Stella's stubbornness with his own to get his way of not letting her out of his sight. When she finally gave up the argument of trying to assure him she was perfectly safe and did not need him hanging around, she stomped over to her desk and called the President of the Toyota plant.

It took a lot of convincing on her part for Mr. Kimoko to see he might be a victim of espionage and to allow her to set up security on his temporary administrative assistant. Once she got the okay from him she called Dave Palmer's security company. Dave was only too glad to help out and send a man out right away. He told her he would have the video and audio set up in a matter of a few hours. Stella called Mr. Kimoko back and arranged to have Elaine out of the office on a false errand for that length of time.

When she was done, she hung up and leaned back in her chair. Everything now depended on Elaine staying true to herself by stealing the confidential information and the case would be solved in a matter of days.

Now all she had to do was find a way to convince George that he did not have to stick to her like glue. She loved him with all that she was but having him hovering around her was unnerving and unnecessary.

As she sat frowning over the problem her brain raced to find a way, George's cell rang.

"Lieutenant Smale," he answered it. After listening to the caller for a few seconds he exploded.

"What the hell do you mean he's gone! You stay right where you are detective, I'll be there in twenty minutes." He slammed his cell phone shut and jammed it in his pocket.

"What happened?" Stella jumped out of her chair.

"That little weasel got around my men and slipped out." He yelled over his shoulder racing to the door.

Stella ran after him and barely made it inside his car when he accelerated and drove off sirens blaring speeding to the safe house. Steering with one hand he reached for the mike hanging below the dash and put out an APB on Jed Bonner.

Stella gripped the dashboard to keep her from flying all over inside the car as he took the corners at top speed. Her stomach wanted to pitch but it wasn't from the fast moving car, it was from the eerie feeling of eyes on her again. What did this Warlock want from her? Why was he so interested in her? If he was enlisted to find Jed then she was making a big mistake by coming along with George.

"George turn the car around and take me to mother's." Suddenly frantic that she might be putting an innocent in peril.

"Stella we're almost there." George kept his eyes on the road.

"I can't go with you. You must take me to mother's and you must go alone. I'm being watched again." She blurted out.

Tires squealed as he slammed on the brakes swerving the car almost hitting a parked car on the side of the road. When the car finally rocked to a stop he turned to look at her. Her face was pale but her eyes held the fire of anger in them. His mind went on fast forward to understand the meaning of her words.

When he caught up to her reasoning, he understood that whoever was watching her would see Jed if they came across him. He threw the gearshift into drive and headed straight for the Manor.

As soon as he screeched to a halt in front of the Manor, he turned to look at her.

"Put your shield up before you go in. If I couldn't get into your office, whoever is watching you from outside will not be able to get in physically or mentally into the Manor. You said the feeling went away after you put the shield up."

Stella agreed jumping out of the car glancing back to watch him speed away. Stella stood bringing enough heat in to perform the spell. She then got down to business of walking around the Manor putting up the shield before she went in.

Of course everyone was there looking like a bunch of frightened gerbils. It appears that Gwen had already told the family about the new Warlock.

Wanda ran over to her wrapping her arms tight around her. Maria held her wand out eyes darting everywhere. Gwen winced in pain holding her head against the overwhelming fear that permeated from everyone gathered there.

Stella grasped her mother's arms firmly and pushed her away releasing the death grip she had on her. Morgana just stood hands folded in front of her waiting for the others to get a grip on themselves.

Stella looked at them all and saw the fear and knew she had to do or say something for her sister's sake. She could see the pain she was suffering.

"Gwen, let go, clear your mind." She shouted over to her. She wasn't getting through to her. Gwen was doubling over with the pain.

Stella shook her mother to try and snap her out of her fear. "Mom, you have to calm down. Now. Morgana," she looked to her cousin, "talk to Maria, get her to calm down, Gwen is suffering."

Morgana quickly walked over to Maria placing her hand on the one Maria was holding the wand in and gently eased it down. The gentleness of her touch got through to Maria and had her taking in the breath she didn't know she'd been holding.

Wanda was a different issue. She had to reach deep down inside and use all her strength to settle her nerves down. Slowly the pain eased away from Gwen. She rose up but still clutched her head. All the heightened

76 S.J SMALE

emotions from the women around her had left her with a huge headache. But at least she didn't feel like she was being split in half now.

Seeing that her sister was no longer in danger Stella left the women to head to the kitchen. She took a seat and waited for the rest of them to follow suit.

When the rest of them followed her in, Morgana forced Maria to sit down knowing she was still too shook up to fuss about the stove without causing herself an injury. Morgana went over and put the kettle on to boil.

Stella decided to give them all time to settle down before diving into the problem at hand. As soon as Morgana made the tea carried it over to the table and sat a cup in front of everyone, she took her seat and waited for Stella to begin.

Stella rubbed her hands over her face then placed them flat on the table. There was no other way to tell them but to come right out with it. But first she had a couple of things to say to her sister.

"Gwen, I'm not sure I should have forced mother and Maria to calm down. You took it upon yourself to tell them about this problem knowing they would be scared out of their skin. How dare you," she glared at her sister. "When are you going to trust me to know what is best? Being the elder daughter doesn't give you the right to upset and frighten our mother and Maria," she chastised her.

"But I saw how frightened you were." Gwen tried to explain. "You sensed a Warlock that is watching you wherever you go. You sense this Warlock has different powers then the others."

"All that is true Gwen, but I asked you to keep your mind on Jed, not me and now he's in the wind and he wouldn't be if you had done what I asked you to do. I'll deal with this other Warlock," she spat at her.

Gwen flew back in her seat as if she'd been landed a physical blow. Stella just told her that it was her fault a human was in terrible danger because she didn't do what she asked her to do. If this human dies, it will be because of her. The guilt of that swamped her and left her speechless. Tears filled her eyes.

Now she turned to the others having dealt with her sister.

"First let me say that before I came in I placed an extra shield around the Manor for added protection." That had all their heads snapping towards her.

"Why would we need extra protection Stella?" Wanda's voice rose in anxiety.

"Because mom, I don't know what we're dealing with at the moment. I can only tell you that I think it is another Warlock like Gwen just said and this one is more powerful than George."

Wanda jumped up from the table but Morgana grabbed her arm and with a very severe warning look forced her to sit back down.

"Stella," Morgana's voice was firm. "I think you better explain to us why you think this and start at the beginning."

Stella nodded her head. She told them how she first felt like someone was watching her and the way she went about finding out it wasn't caused by a human. She explained the reason George ruled out the possibility of it being Geoffrey or Wilfred. She told them everything up to the point where she made George take her here instead of staying with him to go to the safe house.

When she came to the part where the feeling went away after putting up her own shield, the women relaxed a little knowing that they were safe inside the Manor from being watched or overheard by this new development.

Gwen, still filled with guilt, described to the women the feeling Stella had since she felt it too, being inside her head. When Gwen finished, the women sat there stunned for a minute and then they all started talking at once. The volume of their chatter pierced through Stella's head, giving her a headache. When she couldn't take it any longer she pounded her fists on the table causing them all to stop and look at her.

"Is this Warlock stronger than you Stella?" Morgana, always the coolheaded one asked.

"I don't know," Stella wished with all she was that she could have given them a definite no to that question. But until she came face to face with the Warlock she had no idea herself if she was stronger or not.

"I can't figure out what this Warlock wants. Right now all he does is watch me. I keep thinking that he has had ample opportunity to try something but he hasn't. Whether that is a good sign or not, I can't tell."

"Then the only answer is for you to stay here under the protection of the Manor Stella." Wanda insisted reaching for her hand and held it firm. All she wanted was to protect her child.

"Mom, you know I can't do that." Stella placed her other hand over her mother's and squeezed. "Until we know what this Warlock is after, I have to ask all of you to stay here, even you Gwen," she looked at her sister and raised her hand to stop her from arguing. "Gwen you

are gifted but your gifts aren't strong enough to go up against him
alone. I am asking you to do this for me and for mom's sake."

She watched the struggle on her sister's face, wanting to be
independent but knowing in her heart that she was right. Gwen's
shoulders sagged when she finally gave in to reason.

"I will stay on one condition Stella. You promised that I would be
in on capturing Wilfred and I am holding you to that promise."

Gwen could be stubborn but Stella knew the reason behind the
stand she was taking on this point.

"I said I would try to find a way for you to be part of that and I will
keep my word. Thank you Gwen, for agreeing to stay here." She patted
her mother's hand again. "If you can follow this simple instruction at least
it will put mom's mind at rest for one of us, unless of course, you want to
disobey me again and put more people at risk." She narrowed her eyes at
Gwen and watched her flinch and turned and smiled at her mother.

"I would feel a lot better if both my daughters stayed here with me
until this Warlock is found."

"Mom you know I can't do that." Stella leaned over and kissed
her cheek.

"Okay, now if there is anyone you want over here, you had better
call them so I can walk them in and then I have to go."

Maria wanted Gertrude and Tempest. The others shook their
heads. Maria called up her friend while Stella called George to come
and pick her up.

Of course it was only a matter of seconds when Gertrude
appeared outside the door. Stella took her in and told her and her
daughter that the others would fill her in. George took longer since he
had to take the human way of driving there.

On their way over to her office, George filled her in on the
progress of the missing Jed. Apparently he'd jimmied open a window
and slipped out. The APB was out but so far no one has spotted him
yet. George told her that if they didn't find him soon, his chances of
survival were very slim.

"George I'm sorry that my sister let us down and we can't
use magic to bring him in. We already have one man in custody
that knows too much." Stella was referring to Jeffery Ballenger
remembering being transported by Maria from Germany back to
Canada by the use of her wand.

"I know that Stella and Inspector Wise of the RCMP will not close the file on you. We have no option but to bring him in the normal way. I'm just so angry that the stupid fool put himself in jeopardy."

"I know, we might lose him and I am not happy about that either."

"I thought your sister was watching him. Why didn't she call to tell us he was seeking to escape?" George asked her.

Stella thought for a moment on how to tell him. "George, Gwen switched from him to watching me when he made good his escape. She felt if she kept tabs on me it might alert her earlier of immediate danger." Stella shook her head.

"George I don't want this brought up again to Gwen. I've already laid into her and she is very scared and sensitive right now. I guarantee she feels guilty enough about being at fault for this."

"Darling none of this is her fault," he disagreed. "The detail I had on them failed to do their job too. I'm just so sorry that we stretched Gwen so much especially in her fragile state." He frowned.

"She's just got her confidence back and then all this had to happen. I know my sister is strong, but there is just so much one person can handle. I'd hate to see her lose any of that newly found confidence over this. Shoving some blame in her face brought back some anger in her and I think that's given her a bit more strength."

"She is strong and she is with her family right now. I'm sure she will rally with them all there to help her." George glanced over at Stella. Secretly he was angry with Gwen for not doing what Stella asked her. They would have been alerted of his intention of escape had she kept her mind linked with Jeffery.

Stella sat biting her lip now as he drove. George wanted the wedding in a few short weeks, she still had her case to solve and so does he. With so much going on and especially now that someone was watching her, she just didn't see how her and her family could pull it off. Maybe if the wedding was postponed until everything going on around them settled down a bit, then they could relax enough to plan for a wedding.

This was something she knew would only make George angry and more suspicious of her feelings towards him. But damn it, there was just too much for them to deal with at the present.

Now how to find a good way to tell him, she worried her bottom lip.

It was a good thing his concentration was on his driving or he'd have seen her mind working overtime and start questioning her. Right now his mind was on the missing Jed and this new player in the game.

They both feel strongly that Geoffrey and Wilfred are not the ones keeping an eye on Stella. This new player has him very worried. Knowing that Stella is increasing in strength and powers and is becoming less and less dependent on him and his powers didn't stop him from feeling he must protect her. It was getting harder and harder for him to come to terms with the fact his Warlock powers are becoming less needed by her is hitting him very hard. To learn that she was becoming more powerful than him has damaged his ego and making him question himself for the first time in his life.

CHAPTER

Eleven

G eorge dropped Stella off at her office and went back to work. Stella walked into her office feeling oddly uneasy. On the drive back to her office she didn't sense anyone watching her. The last time she sensed it was on the drive to the Manor. She put in a call to her mom to check that the shield was still holding up. Her mother answered the phone and assured her that they were all fine.

Relieved that no one was in danger, she got down to writing up her notes on the case she was working on. Her nerves must have been strung tight, because when the phone rang she jumped.

"Stella Blake Investigator," she answered.

"Oh Stella you sound so funny," Deb giggled on the other end.

"Thanks, I live to amuse you. What can I do for you?" Stella was trying to get her heart rate back to normal.

"Oh, oh Stella you should see it," then she laughed again. "But of course you can't see it 'cause it's here and you're there."

Deb's giggles were contagious, making Stella smile. "You're right I can't see it. Now do you want to tell me what we're talking about or do I have to guess. Busy here Deb."

"Not too busy for this. You have to come over right away for a fitting. It's your wedding dress, silly." Deb peeled into giggles again.

"Like I said Deb, busy here." Stella shuddered just thinking what it must look like. A vision of strutting down the aisle looking like an ostrich or peacock came to mind.

"Uh-uh, you promised you'd come for a fitting. Well it's ready for it now." Stella could just see the little heart shaped mouth pouting. "You can take five minutes out of your day. This is important." Stella now envisioned Deb stomping her tiny little foot.

'Yeah,' Stella thought, 'like my job isn't important.' But she did promise and she never could stand up to a righteous Debra Styles pout.

"Okay, okay, I'll be there as soon as I can." Stella caved.

"Okay-dokey, see you in a few minutes." Deb hung up on a peal of giggles.

Stella was sure there was no one in the known universe that could refuse that little imp. She closed her notebook and left the office wishing she was going into battle with a dozen Warlocks instead of the horrors of a dress fitting session.

Visions of what concoction Deb had dreamed up for her to wear on her wedding day had her trembling in fear. She saw feathers sprouting out all over with blinding sparkling sequences glittering everywhere. She shuddered. Remembering her friend's latest fashion show she prayed there were no wings attached to the gown.

Realizing there was no getting out of it, she grudgingly walked out of the office. Scuffling her feet, she made her way over to her car, got in and slowly drove over to the nightmare awaiting for her.

Stella pulled up in front of Deb's home. She took a deep breath before climbing out of the car bracing herself for what she deemed was going to be a fate worse than death.

Stella was shown in and told to go right up. Miss Styles was waiting for her in her studio. Stella thanked the housekeeper and headed up to meet her fate.

She stopped just outside the room watching her friend flit around the room with a tape measure draped around her neck, a pad full of colourful pins wrapped around her tiny wrist. She had her long curly blond hair pulled back and held there by tiny little butterfly hairpins. Her lavender eyes glowing as she darted from table to mannequin.

Stella's eyes stopped tracing her movements when she glimpsed the creation covering the mannequin. Her mouth popped open at the sheer beauty of the gown. The single thin strap was covered in emerald and diamond chips. The sweetheart bodice was outlined in shimmering silver. The waist boasted a band of glistening crystals. The white gown flowed out from the waist in soft billowing layers of satin and lace. The layered satin folds gathered gave the impression of soft puffy clouds were held in place by tiny three tier droplets of tiny pearls. The long train swept down in the same billowing clouds. It was the most beautiful gown she had ever seen.

This was a dress dreams were made of. She knew in that moment that no other woman in the world would ever have a dress to compare with it. It took her breath away.

Tears ran down her cheeks, she was so moved by it. How could she have thought for one moment that Deb would make anything but the perfect gown for her? And it was. It was perfect. It was a dream dress. She was ashamed for not trusting her friend to make something that was exactly right for her.

The sudden squeal had Stella taking her eyes off the dress just in time to find her arms filled with the tiny little genius. Deb gave her a hard squeeze before letting her go. She grabbed her arm and pulled her into the room.

"Okay strip," Deb was riding on a high from catching the look on Stella's face when she saw the gown. She walked over to the mannequin and began to carefully remove it.

Stella slowly began to undress still stunned by the beauty. She wanted to tell Deb how she felt about the gown but knew if she spoke she'd burst out crying. She could see herself in it already.

Deb began tapping her little foot showing her impatience with her. Finally when Stella was down to her bra and panties, Deb walked over ordered Stella to bend down so she could slip it over her head.

The feel of the dress next to her body was euphoric. It felt like a second skin so soft and luxurious. It fit her perfectly. It was just a touch too long making that the only alteration needed. Deb walked her over to the floor length mirror and watched her reaction to the mirror image. Deb expected a happy face, a glowing accolade to her creation. She didn't expect the tears that freely ran down her friend's face.

"You don't like it?" The disappointment hit her hard.

"Oh God Deb, it's the most beautiful gown I've ever seen. I look like a queen. I've never had anything so beautiful before in my life and you did this for me. Versace, Dior or Chanel could never create such absolute perfect beauty your brilliant mind has created." She buried her face in her hands and just let her emotions take over.

"I don't deserve anything this beautiful, I'm not worthy," Stella got out between sobs. "I'm an awful friend and a selfish person. I don't deserve to wear this wonderful creation. This gown is fit for a Queen, not me." She sobbed.

Deb's face lit up. "What, did you think, that I'd put feathers or seaweed on you for your wedding day? You should know by now that I know exactly what suits you and what doesn't. " She bubbled with laughter so pleased that Stella liked it after all.

"Oh Deb I'm so sorry. You are a genius and yes you do know me." She hugged her friend.

"Of course I do silly," she wiggled out of her arms.

"Now stand still while I pin up the hem then you can get out of it before you get it all wet from your tears. Stand up straight."

Deb got busy with her tape measure and pins. It didn't take the little sprite long before she had the hem pinned up and was helping her out of it.

The gown felt so good on her she hated to have to take it off. After she quickly got dressed again, she helped Deb to put the gown back on the mannequin again.

"I've made the veil and the train can be attached for the ceremony and taken off for the reception. But you don't need to see the veil yet," she paused. "Stella you don't know what it means to me for you to let me do this for you. I know my fashions aren't your style but you are my best friend in the whole wide world. Thank you for letting me create this for you." Now her eyes were all watery.

"Deb you are my best friend too and I am so sorry I ever doubted you. I will never doubt you again when it comes to what suits me." Now they both wept as they hugged each other.

That's how Richard found them when he walked in. The two of them hugging and rocking each other and crying. It shocked him at first thinking something was seriously wrong, but then he spotted the tiny smile on his love's face. He shook his head. Women, he thought. He'd never understand them. But he was smart enough to escape unnoticed before they dragged him into the hormonal estrogen filled minefield.

Stella stayed for awhile enjoying some time with her friend before heading·back to the office. It was wonderful to sit around relaxed talking about silly stuff and letting go of all the worries and problems she knew were waiting for her once she left. She also wanted to stay longer just to stare at the most magnificent wedding gown in the world and it was all hers.

Debra was better than a doctor's prescription. She arrived with dark circles under her eyes and worry lines furrowing her brow. When she left he was simply glowing with awe and joy. Her mind filled with a vision of how she looks in her wedding gown and the look on George's face when he watches her walk down the aisle towards him.

She even forgot about the reason she came up with to postpone the wedding. Just seeing the dress and spending time with her friend was like a mini vacation for her.

Deb was already planning her next collection and ran some ideas by her friend. Apparently working on the wedding gown had put some fresh ideas in her mind. This time it seemed she was fixated on the theme of clouds. Stella didn't know how anyone could make clothes that reminded people of clouds, but then if anyone could, it would be her friend. She couldn't wait to see this one.

Stella decided to drive over to the Manor before heading back to the office. As soon as she turned onto Main Street the feeling of being watched swept over her. Anger filled her. She'd had enough of this and decided she had to do something to drive this Warlock into the open. Instead of heading to the Manor, she turned the next corner and made her way to Waterworks Park.

She made a slow circle of the park before parking the car.

Stella remained in the car drumming her fingers on the steering wheel. The sensation of being watched stayed with her. Looking through the windows she searched the area for anyone paying any particular attention to her.

The park was almost deserted at this time of day. A few mothers strolling·about with their babies in strollers, a couple of school kids ditching school. There were a couple of older men sitting at a picnic table enjoying a game of chess. The rest of the park was left to the animals that claimed this area as their home.

Climbing out of the car, she made her way over to one of the small wooden bridges spanning the many man-made ponds filled with water lilies and golden carp.

She tried to get a fix on the direction the sensation was coming from. Bracing herself on the railing of the bridge she closed her eyes and tried to concentrate, focusing her energy.

Now that there were no distractions around her, flashes of a face popped in and out of her mind, long black hair, startling aqua blue-green eyes. She caught the sense that this person was powerfully built. If it wasn't for the colour of the eyes that flashed in her mind, she would have thought she was seeing George. She pushed her mind to hold the image but as soon as she did, it was gone and so was the sensation of being watched.

Stella's eyes flew open. She spun around looking everywhere hoping to get a glimpse of the Warlock. There was no doubt in her mind now that it was a Warlock that was watching her. She scanned all the bushes shrubs and trees hoping to catch a movement that would tell her where he was.

Nothing.

It didn't make sense to her. Here she was in the open alone, yet he made no move on her. Why was he watching her? What did he hope to see or learn? Why not come after her when she was a perfect target unprotected as far as he knew?

Stella remained where she was for another twenty minutes but whoever was watching her wasn't doing so now. She made her way back to the car and drove to the Manor.

Wanda opened the door as soon as Stella reached it. She could see the worried look on her mother's face. Stella bent down and kissed her cheek and put an arm around her as they walked back to the kitchen.

As soon as they walked in she noticed cousin Morgana had them all busy with the wedding plans to help take their minds off their troubles. The table was once again filled with papers of seating arrangements and lists. Little swatches of materials were strewn over the table as well.

Gwen, Maria, Gertrude, Tempest and Morgana looked up as soon as they entered. Stella merely shook her head indicating there was no new information. For now she was going to keep her failed attempt to draw him into the open to herself. Knowing the women in her family, they would only panic and make more out of it than there was.

Maria brought Stella a cup of tea as the rest all took their seats again. To help ease the tension, Stella described the gown that Deb made for her. It did the trick, worry was replaced by excitement. They pelted her with more questions about the gown. How did it look on her? How did it feel? It was worth the agony of girly talk to have them focus on that instead of the Warlock.

Stella left them in a lighter mood. She drove back to her office and felt relieved that the watcher was leaving her alone, for now.

It had been a long day and a stress filled one. Stella's head kept bobbing as she struggled to keep her eyes open to finish up her work. She decided to rest her head on the desk just for a minute. A blast of noise had her jumping out of her chair reaching for her gun. She blinked her eyes to get them to focus. Realizing she must have fallen asleep, she made her way slowly to the door. The noise was coming from the other side. It sounded like she was under attack. Gun ready, she carefully peeked out of the window. The thought of Warlocks attacking her put her whole system on full alert. Her heartbeat raced, she readied the heat in case she needed to transform. But what she saw had her lower the gun. It was a Warlock but this one wasn't attacking. It was George trying to get her attention to let him in. She had forgotten about her shield not allowing any magic in without her help.

Stella holstered her gun and opened the door to a very annoyed Warlock. She took hold of his hand and led him in.

"Stella I don't like this." His eyes flashed with anger. "What if you were in danger and I couldn't get in to help you. You could trip and knock yourself unconscious. Then what would you do? You're isolated here and I don't like it."

Telling her she was unable to take care of herself had her anger rising. Her green eyes turned to ice, piercing him where he stood.

"I have taken care of myself all my life. I was doing very well on my own before I met you. I never needed anyone's help." Stella fisted her hands planting them firmly on her hips as she went toe to toe with him. "How dare you come in here and tell me I'm a helpless female and cannot take care of myself." Sticking her finger in his chest, "you could not get in here without my help if you remember." Sparks were shooting from her eyes now. A wind began to swirl around her making her hair fly in all directions. Stella was unaware of the change going on in her she was so filled with righteous anger.

George could feel the heat coming off her. He took a giant step back to avoid getting singed. His anger vanished in the face of hers. His bloody ego was about to pay a heavy price if he did not get her to calm down. It was just that he was so worried after she didn't answer his calling for her outside. He imagined all kinds of terrible reasons for it. Now if he did not get her to calm down, she would not have to worry about the shield protecting her home. She was about to burn that home down all by herself.

Taking a huge leap of faith, he stepped toward her and tried to rub her arm, getting his hands blistering for his effort. He darted back a few steps. The pain of the burns showed clearly in his eyes as he winced.

Stella saw the pain and instantly felt repulsed at having caused it. Immediately the wind and heat died as she rushed to him.

"Oh God, what have I done?" She tried to take his hands to inspect the injury making him wince again and suck in his breath.

His hands were the source of his gifts and she hurt them. She would never forgive herself. She had to help him. Stella left him and ran into her quarters to get the first aid kit.

George tried to stop her but she ignored him. All she could think of now was to get something to help him. When she returned, she found him sitting in one of the chairs calmly sipping on a cup of coffee like nothing had ever happened. She stood in the middle of the room gaping at him, holding the first aid kit in her hand.

"Darling I tried to tell you that medical aid was quite unnecessary." He smiled up at her.

"But your hands . . ."

"Are perfectly fine thank you." He lifted one hand wiggling his fingers.

"Oh," Surprised, but very relieved, she walked over and sat behind her desk placing the first aid kit on it.

CHAPTER

Twelve

N ow that both their tempers had cooled down, they looked at each other sheepishly. Both of them apologized to each other for letting their emotions get out of control.

After witnessing the power she displayed in a blink of an eye, George vowed to keep his ego in check from now on. It was very clear that Stella could most certainly take care of herself.

Once their apologies were done, they got down to the business of the missing Jed and Stella told him about her experience and revelations in the park.

"Do you think that was wise to try and take on this unknown Warlock by yourself?" George quickly held up his hands at the flash of anger in her eyes. "I have every confidence that you can cope on your own, Stella. But not knowing the kind of power this one has, I don't think I'm out of line asking the question."

He was right, she knew he was right and that doused most of the anger. But for some reason it still grated her.

"But I won't know how powerful he is until I face him. What does he want? Why is he so interested in just me?" It unnerved her that she couldn't find an answer.

This puzzle had no pieces to it.

"We do know that he cannot watch you inside your shield and that is something at least."

"Yeah, I suppose so."

"Please don't get angry with me Stella, but we both know that you can be attacked outside your office. I can't help but worry about that." George tried to explain as gently as he could.

"George, this person has had many chances to come at me but hasn't. That is the problem I'm facing. Why not do something instead of simply watch me? This just doesn't make any sense to me."

"You're thinking this magic is not part of Geoffrey and Wilfred's plan?" He asked.

"How can it be if this magic isn't making any moves against me?" Stella tried to line up the evidence.

"Darling it has been a long day. Why don't we call it a night and see if tomorrow will bring us some answers."

At the mention of sleep, Stella's face flushed. That was the reason she didn't hear him calling her. She had fallen asleep at her desk.

George cocked an eyebrow at the blush blooming in her cheeks. Stella shook her head got up and led them into her private quarters.

Stella spent a dreamless night nestled warm and snug against George and woke up feeling refreshed and ready to face the day. She smelled the coffee first and finding herself alone in bed knew George was busy in the kitchen. She climbed out of bed showered and dressed quickly then following the aroma made a beeline to the kitchen to get her caffeine fix.

George loved the way her long wet red hair hung down her back to dry naturally. Her red bangs combed straight to slip just below the top of her arched eyebrows. He watched her make her way over to the table sit down and take the first sip of her morning coffee. The gun and holster didn't deter the lust building in him just looking at her always caused.

His eyes began to glaze over with the lust. He made a move to go to her just as the phone rang. Stella's head came up at the sound and caught the look in his eyes. Her face pinked up at the intensity of it.

She felt the punch of it hit causing her glands to go into overdrive. She got up to answer the phone and was embarrassed even more by the huskiness in her voice.

"Sorry to bother you Lieutenant," Sergeant Connelly stammered. "I tried reaching Lieutenant Smale at his home but didn't get an answer. I was wondering if you knew where he is. It's kind of important."

The sound of the Sergeant's nervous voice had her quickly regain her composure.

"Yes Sergeant, he's right here." Stella handed the phone to George.

"What is it Sergeant?" George forgot all about his previous intentions toward Stella and became all cop as he listened intently to the stammering Sergeant.

"Yes Sir, Lieutenant Sir," Sergeant Connelly couldn't help it, the new Lieutenant always made him nervous. "I just thought you'd want to know that we located Jed Bonner Sir."

George stood very still. "Is he in custody?" Instinctively he knew that the little thief was no longer among the living.

"Uh, well, in a way Sir. He's being transported to the morgue now. Sorry Sir."

"I see," George sighed. "I want you to call the morgue and request that Dr. Ballard be put in charge of the body. I'll be in shortly, thank you Sergeant." George hung up on the nervous man.

He turned to Stella. "They found our young criminal dead."

"Yeah so I gathered from the conversation. How did he die?"

"I won't know until I go in." He walked over to her cupping her face in his hands leaned down and softly kissed her lips. "I'm sorry Stella; we lost our chance to bring the two into the open."

"I'm coming with you." She stepped away and headed for the door.

They drove over to the morgue together, neither one saying a word both busy with their own thoughts. George pulled into the parking lot and parked in the slot reserved for police. Silently they got out of the car walked into the building and down the white painted hallway towards the autopsy room. Their steps echoed off the pristine walls making an eerie sound.

George was glad to see Dr. Ballard waiting for them in his clear plastic coat covering a grey pinstripe suit. He peered at them over glasses that hung halfway down his nose. He wasn't humming or smiling.

For the first time since she could remember, Stella noticed that there was no music playing in the background. Dr. Ballard always worked with his favourite music playing softly in the room. It was like a ritual with him, soothing him as he worked. He believed in being very respectful to the people brought to him to find the answers that ended their lives.

On the table beside him lay the remains of Jed Bonner not looking his best.

"Dr. Ballard," George greeted him.

"Lieutenant, Lieutenant," he addressed them both. To him Stella would always be Lieutenant no matter what profession she chose to work.

"I can tell you both, right now, that I don't like this." He indicated with a jerk of his head towards the body. "This is the third time I've had someone come in to me in this condition and I don't like it."

They watched his face redden in anger. "From what I'm looking at, your kind do not have any compassion in them for them to do something this horrendous. I hoped never to see this done to anyone again."

"Doc," Stella spoke softly hiding her own anger. "We told you there are good and bad in our kind the same as yours. Hitler was human and you know what he did. We are trying to find the ones responsible for this." Suggesting Hitler was human was a lie but she felt it better not to mention that to him.

"Well, I suggest you look harder." He yelled at them. He knew these two did not cause the condition the poor lad was in and knew too that his own compassion was getting in the way of objectivity. He pinched the bridge of his nose with his thumb and forefinger attempting to gain some self control.

"I apologize for the outburst. I have seen just about everything one person can do to another in my line of work. But this is beyond and apparently it is causing me to lose some of my objectivity."

"There is no need to apologize Dr. we realize and appreciate you are working under extreme circumstances. Keeping our secret is an added burden on you. I promise you the ones responsible will be dealt with." George walked over to stand beside him.

Dr. Ballard could not help feeling just a little nervous standing so close to them knowing what he now knows about them.

"It is not something I could tell anyone unless I want to lose the respect of my colleagues' or worse, lose my license and career." He snorted.

"Just do me a favour and catch the ones doing this before another body comes to me in this condition." He ordered. "Now if the two of you don't mind I'd like to get on with my work. This poor boy needs my full attention." Dr. Ballard moved away to put some space between him and them and gather the instruments needed.

They left the good doctor to get on with his work. George dropped Stella off at her house and left her there to head over to his office and read the report on Jed's death.

Stella kept thinking about the strain and pressure they put on Dr. Ballard's shoulders in getting him to, not only know about them, but to keep what he learned a secret.

His mind thought in the linear of strict pure science. Stella knew that not being a particularly religious man, it was very hard for him to even contemplate the idea of thinking another way. But even if he could magic would never enter his thought process. All the time she knew him from her days on the Force, Doctor Ballard's reports were golden for the Crown. Just like she always got a conviction for her cases from her intense hard work, the Crown relied on Doctor Ballard's reports to back up her findings.

Stella had never heard of anyone questioning his findings for the Crown. In some way she considered him a good partner at that time. He was meticulous in his ethics and his work and a credit to the Police Force. It was his absolute faith in science and strong ethics that proved his reliability and excellent accounting of the facts for the Crown to prove his cases.

It just made her sad that she had to burst his scientific beliefs. Dr. Ballard always put his faith in science. This made more sense to him. Believing in something you couldn't see smell or touch was just not to be considered. He supposed that religion and a belief in some invisible higher being made others feel comfortable and gave meaning to their lives and the situations people found themselves in, but finding answers with concrete facts that can be proven by data and science was more of a comfort for him.

Dr. Ballard never thought of himself as an atheist, but as a scientist. Atheism to him was another religion, one that was anti-God. Ones who believed in God also believed in the concept of a Devil. He never believed in the so called miracles. To him, everything that happens in this world must be analyzed and have an explanation based on facts that can be proven. So called miracles are not proof of anything but a form of mass hypnosis.

Having the two of them not only tell him there is magic in this World but to actually show him in a way he cannot deny has thrown him off his game a bit. This has him questioning his own belief in true science.

After the meeting with the two of them he tried everything he knew to dispute what his eyes witnessed. Magic, to him, was a simple case of misdirection to fool an audience and for the most part mass hypnosis. But sitting in his office with no mirrors and no smoke, his brain could find no way to prove a logical explanation. This is what is giving him the most problem. No area of science would ever explain what his eyes saw.

CHAPTER

Thirteen

B ack in her office, Stella decided it was time to search Elaine's background again to see if she frequented any particular stores or restaurants. From some of the clothes she saw strewn about the apartment, Elaine had very expensive tastes.

Her credit check showed a penchant for high-end stores, five-star restaurants, and the girl enjoyed the theater. She checked the dates the theater tickets were charged to on her credit card and matching them up with shows, she found out she was particularly fond of musicals. Stella reached for the paper and flipped through to the entertainment section. Momma Mia was scheduled to perform next week.

Stella hoped that the surveillance she had Dave install at the Toyota plant would catch her in the act of taking confidential papers out of there. Should that happen she could go after her and bring her in. Knowing the incriminating evidence was still in her apartment and could not be used since she found them illegally, had her hedging her bets on getting her one way or the other.

With the incriminating evidence on the tapes the police could get a warrant to search her apartment and the Crown would have a slam dunk case against her.

Everything depended on her being caught red-handed on the surveillance tapes.

Even if Elaine somehow got wind of what was happening, Stella knew right where to find her. She'd never resist attending the musical show. Now it was just a waiting game.

Since she figured that she'd found everything she could on Elaine, Stella decided to put Mr. Yamada's case aside and concentrate on finding a way to bring Geoffrey and his son out into the open.

George said he could sense another Warlock but had to be in the same area to do that. That meant that the two were staying out of range. Maybe it was time for her and George to take a little field trip, she thought.

Stella got out a map and began charting out routes they would take. Because they were doing a hit and run she figured they'd need to be close but not close enough to alert George's radar. Stella decided to extend the boundary out to a hundred kilometer radius. It didn't make sense for them to be further out than that.

She began writing down locations she felt might suit the needs of the renegade father and son. This at least was pro-active. Sitting around waiting for them to hit again was not an option for her and just wasn't her style.

Stella knew once they did get close enough for George to sense them then they would have to back away quickly or run the chance of being detected. That would at least tell them where they were located and they could set up some kind of surveillance in order to catch their movements. It was a big chance but as far as she could see it was the only chance they had of stopping them.

If there was a way she could find them on her own she would do it and not take George away from his work. But only a full Warlock can sense another full Warlock. She needed George for this.

Stella reached for the phone to call George, but before she picked it up, it rang.

"Blake Private Investigator," Stella answered.

"Hey Stella," Dave's friendly voice was on the other end. "Glad I caught you in."

"What's up Dave?"

"Well I got good news and bad news for ya,"

"I could use some good news about now," Stella sat back in her chair.

"Okay, the surveillance worked and we caught her on tape red-handed." He waited.

"You got Elaine taking copies of confidential papers home?" She sat back up in her chair.

"We got her making copies, putting them in her purse and walking out of her office with them, yes."

Stella frowned. "And the bad news?"

"Yeah, well all I can say is it's a small world. She walked into her office as my man was coming out of it with the tapes. Here's the thing, Stella, she recognized him."

"Oh my God, what are the chances? How did your man handle it?"

"He told her he'd been working out of town for awhile, just got back in a few days ago and heard she was working there, thought he'd drop in to say hi."

"And did she buy it?"

"Stella, he's real good at reading people. According to him, she didn't buy it for a minute. I'm sorry Stella, but I think your girl is on to us."

"Okay Dave, thanks. If she takes off she'll probably go back to her apartment and get rid of the evidence I found there. Send the tapes over and I'll take it from here."

"I'm really sorry Stella."

"Hey don't beat yourself up Dave. It's like you said, it's a small world. Things like this are bound to happen once in awhile. I have an idea where I can find her. Send the tapes to me and I'll see the police get them."

"I'll messenger them over now. You can be sure I'll make it a policy from now on to know who my people are acquainted with. This won't happen again, I promise."

"Don't sweat it Dave. I still consider you the best in the business." Stella tried to ease some of the disappointment in him.

After she hung up from Dave, she called George. They made plans to meet up at Robin's Nest for dinner. Next she called Mr. Yamada and Mr. Kimoko to let them know she now had proof and the thief would be apprehended soon. Each one thanked her for her success. She heard the relief in Mr. Yamada's voice. His faith in his employees' loyalty was once again restored. Somehow Stella sensed that that was a smidgeon more important to him than having his designs stolen.

She completed her report up to the point of Elaine's capture and filed it away. Now that this case was practically closed, Stella got up to go to her crime board and take down and wipe off everything that had to do with the espionage.

She stood looking at the other board filled with the events and directions of Wilfred and Geoffrey. She circled their names and drew a line down from it where she wrote the word LOCATION with a question mark.

It was time to get down to planning how to deal with them. Finding them was one thing, getting them to go where she and George could deal with them was another. Then there was the problem of Gwen's participation in their capture and keeping her safe.

Stella paced the room trying to think up different scenarios' that might work. Her mind ran over different locations that would be safe from being seen by humans, empty warehouses and factories. But these were close to roads where a passerby might glimpse some activity that would catch their attention. No they simply could not deal with them in the open city.

Suddenly it came to her. They'd have to get the two into the clearing just beyond the woods from her mother's home. The surrounding forest would hide any magical activity and it was private property.

It was a start. The first problem was finding them and the second one is how to get them to the clearing. She would need some bait. Her stomach tightened at the thought, but her sister did insist on helping. She was the only one Wilfred would be willing to go after. He knew Wanda might see him and send up a warning, George is always too close to me for him to try for me. Gwen was the easy one in his mind. They didn't know about my powers yet or they would not still be playing their games.

Stella met George at the restaurant with a smile on her face. It lifted her spirits to have a plan forming even if all the details were not worked out yet.

They walked in together and were shown to a table for two in front of the fireplace. It seemed that tonight was a popular night at Robin's Nest as the restaurant was more than half full. Stella let George order for them both. Her mind was far too busy organizing steps they should take on the upcoming trip.

George picked up on her preoccupation. He didn't miss much when it came to her. He ordered the food and wine to go with it, and then turned his attention on Stella when their waitress left. He waited until she finished whatever was going through her mind and then reached across and placed his hand over hers.

She looked up into his blue eyes. "Sorry, I was thinking."

"Yes you were. Would you care to let me know what all that thinking is about?"

"A trip."

"Are you going on a trip?" His eyebrows winged up.

"We are going on a trip." She corrected.

"Ah, and do you have any particular place in mind? And why and where exactly are we going?" George leaned back in his chair eyeing her carefully.

"Let's just call it a reconnaissance mission. I figure we could do a sweep no more than a hundred kilometer radius from the city."

"Oh, only a hundred kilometer radius, she says," His eyes narrowed as his voice lowered. "Do you realize how much travelling that will involve and how long it will take?"

"We won't be doing the whole area all at once." Stella's eyes flashed. "I've mapped it out. We'll do it in sections."

"And what exactly are we looking for on these trips?" He thought he knew and if he was right and something went wrong they could be risking deadly consequences for their efforts.

"We both know those two murderers are not in this area or you would have sensed them. They're somewhere outside the area but close enough to get in and out quickly. I figure if we find the section they're in with your radar system we could come up with a plan to take them there or draw them to where we want them."

"You are forgetting one important fact Stella, if I can sense them, they can sense me."

"No I didn't forget that. I figure the moment you sense them we turn around and leave. They won't know it's you, they might think it's another Warlock just passing through."

"That's pretty slim. Have you considered what they'll do if they realize it is me they sense Stella? You would be putting your family and Naomi's in great danger."

"Well hell," Stella knew she and her family could probably take care of themselves, but she had totally forgotten about Naomi.

When their food arrived, Stella sat pushing it around on her plate, her appetite was gone. She thought she was so clever, that she had come up with a pretty good plan only to have it squashed like a bug. If it wasn't for Naomi she would still consider going for it.

George coaxed her into eating a little before paying for the meal and following her back to her place. They parked in her driveway and walked up to find Dave waiting just outside the door.

"Hey Stella, George," Dave greeted them. "Did you put a new security system on your place?" He rubbed the fingers on his right hand.

"Oh, yeah, I did," Stella watched him nursing his fingers. "Are you okay?"

"Yeah, still have all five digits," he wiggled his fingers at her. "I've never seen a system like this. You'll have to tell me all about it. Maybe I can find a use for it."

Stella had to think fast. "Oh, well sure but as you see I haven't got all the bugs worked out of it yet. When I do I'll let you know. Is there some reason you came over?" Stella walked past him opened the door and led them all in.

She went over to the coffee maker and poured them all a coffee before taking her seat behind her desk. George and Dave took a seat across from her.

"I was on my way to Louise's and thought I'd stop in to give you a bit of information that came my way." He took a sip of his coffee.

"It seems Elaine Farmer got wind that it was you looking into her and responsible for setting up the surveillance on her. After viewing the tapes you sent to the police, they got a warrant and searched her apartment. I'm afraid any evidence you found there was gone when they searched and so is she. They've issued an APB on her."

"Thanks Dave. I underestimated her intelligence. Apparently she's a lot smarter than I thought." She tapped her fingers on the desk. "If the police don't pick her up in the next few days, I have a lead on where I might find her."

"Sorry, Stella, if it wasn't for her recognizing my man she might have been under arrest by now."

"Don't worry about it Dave. These things happen. It's not your fault or your man's fault either. He was quick on his feet to have an answer ready for her when she questioned him."

"I've got the rest of my crew writing down everyone they know so we don't run into this problem again."

"That's good Dave, that's why you're the best in the business." Stella wanted to reassure him of her confidence in him.

"Well I better get over to Louise before she sends out a search party," he put his cup down on the desk got up waved at them both making his way over to the door.

"Oh, Dave," Stella suddenly had an idea pop in her head. "I wonder if you could do me a favour. There's a musical playing next week. I was wondering if you could work your magic and cop me two tickets to 'Momma Mia'."

George looked at her like she had just blown a fuse. He knew musicals were not her choice in theater productions. In fact he knew she couldn't stand them.

"Sure no problem Stella, and thanks for understanding the snafu. See ya both later." He walked out feeling better than when he came in.

"Stella, you hate musicals. What's going on?" He frowned at her.

She wiggled her eyebrows at him. "I don't like them but our little Miss Farmer happens to love them. According to her financials, she hasn't missed a single one."

"Ah, now it's making sense. And you are not going to inform the police of this?" A smirk played on his mouth for the fact that he is the police.

"Look George, I know I should call it in, but Dave feels so bad about mucking my case up that I want to take her in for his sake. Maybe if I did that, it wouldn't sting him so much."

"Okay, I'll let it go seeing as how you are taking a member of the police with you to the theater."

"There you go," she wiggled her brows at him again and smiled.

Watching her lean back in her chair, he knew the levity was gone as he watched a frown begin to form. She was back concentrating on the other problem that faced them.

"Stella, I know you want to go hunt for Geoffrey and Wilfred. I also know the safety of Naomi and her brother are holding you back. We'll figure it out, I promise." He wished she didn't look so worried.

"Let's sleep on it tonight and see what the morning brings." He got up walked around to take her hands in his and kissed them.

"George we have to find a way to find those two," she said sadly. "I refuse to allow them to hurt another human."

"On that we both agree on. I just don't understand how I'm not picking up on them when they enter the city," he frowned.

"Yeah, that has me puzzled too. Do you think they've come up with a spell or something that hides them from your senses?" she asked.

"I've never heard of one, but I won't rule that out." He told her. He'd thought of this and was surprised that Stella was thinking along the same lines as him.

She knew there was nothing more she could do tonight and let him guide her into her quarters and to bed. It surprised George how fast she drifted off to sleep with everything on her mind.

He stayed awake watching her for awhile. So much was going on around her including the increasing changes to her gifts. George couldn't help swelling with pride on how well she was adjusting to each and every change to her powers. Stella was the strongest woman he'd ever known. A lesser being with magic would have folded under the pressure of so many rapid changes.

Watching her strength shining through each and every time simply undid him and made him love her even more. Finally he allowed himself to slip into sleep.

CHAPTER

Fourteen

*H*er dreams were a mish mash of people and places. She was running down a long white narrow hallway. There were doors on either side down the length of it. Sensing some form of urgency to find something, she began opening them one at a time as she came to them.

The first room contained two people taking photographs of papers that covered a long table. Neither of them looked up as she entered. This wasn't the room she needed.

The next room was filled with bodies lying in various stages of an autopsy on tables stacked up to the ceiling. She quickly backed out and went on to the next door.

The next few rooms were empty. She crossed the hall and started searching through rooms on that side. She found a room full of people drinking and celebrating. Most of the rooms on this side were empty as well.

When she opened the last door she was met with a blast of heat. The room was filled with an eerie grey smoke. Someone inside the smoke was laughing, but the sound of it caused the hairs on the back of her neck to stand up.

As hard as she tried she could not peer through the smoke. She tried to transform but the heat wouldn't build in her no matter how hard she tried.

Instinct told her to run and she did. She ran for all she was worth but the hallway kept stretching and stretching keeping her from reaching its end.

Suddenly she found herself in the clearing in the woods behind her mother's home. As she glanced around she saw bodies lying on the ground. She walked slowly over to them. A sinking feeling crept over her as she neared the bodies. She looked down and found they were the bodies of her family. She opened her mouth to scream when a hand clamped over it silencing her scream. With terrified eyes she glanced up to see the man she saw in her mind at the park. She stood frozen until he whispered in her ear. 'It does not have to be this way.'

Something snapped in her and she began struggling to get free. She had to get free or die. She clawed and punched and punched and punched as he yelled at her to stop. . . .

"Stella stop it. Stop it now." George held her arms that were flying wildly. It was the sudden punch to his gut that woke him. He knew she was trapped in a nightmare fighting for her life. Terror struck his heart. If he couldn't bring her back she might be lost to him forever. He shook her hard all the time yelling for her to stop struggling.

It was no good. Finally he drew her in holding her tight against his body with one arm and slapped her face hard hoping to snap her out of it.

When her struggles lessened he knew she was surfacing from the nightmare. Her eyes fluttered open. Her body soaked in sweat. She went limp in his arms. Now he rocked her and laid kisses on her damp face still holding her tight. His heart beat again knowing she was back, that she didn't leave him.

Stella turned her head and buried her face in his chest breathing in his scent. She began to cry, "Oh God they're all dead. They're all dead and I couldn't save them. My family is dead, they're all dead." Tears poured out as her body wracked with the strength of her crying.

"Hush my darling, your family is not dead. They are fine. It was just a dream." He reassured her over and over again. "Stella you must listen to me," he tilted her head up to look at him. "Your family is alive, it was just a dream." He rained soft kisses over her face.

"Oh God it was so real George. He was there, George, the Warlock I told you about was there. He told me it didn't have to be this way. My family was lying on the ground all dead and it felt so real," her eyes welled up again.

"But you know now it wasn't real. It was just a dream." He insisted.

"George I think it was more than that. I think it was him warning me or offering me something. I'm not sure yet, but I know it wasn't just a dream."

George frowned. He didn't like where this was going. If somehow this Warlock could break through her shield into her subconscious she'd be at his mercy and he couldn't save her.

"If what you're saying is true, and I don't like it at all. Did you get a sense that this Warlock who did that to your family?"

Stella drew away from George and thought about what he asked. Her brows knitted in concentration. She rubbed her wet face with her hands then looked over at him.

"No, he didn't do it. I can't explain how I know but I just do. He didn't kill my family." That revelation had her feeling a bit better. "Who is this Warlock?" She shook her head. "Maybe I've been thinking of him too much and that's why he ended up in my dreams."

George kept his thoughts to himself on that matter. He was going to do whatever he could to find out for himself who this strange Warlock was. Getting into Stella's dreams and causing her pain was one more reason he wanted to go one on one with him.

He was careful to bank his anger from showing. Stella was vulnerable right now and he did not want to cause any more upset to her. He drew her back into his arms and held her drinking in the relief that she was back with him and safe, for now.

He still could not get over the sick feeling that this Warlock was other, was more. For him not to be able to sense him told him he was not in this area. But he'd never known a Warlock to have such a power as to be able to stretch out his mind to see in a different area than he's in, has never been heard of before. This filled him with worry that they were dealing with something new and unrecorded throughout the centuries.

This was an unknown power. George's entire being filled with fear for Stella, for her family and for the rest of the magic beings. For all they knew Stella was the only being that was other than the rest of them. Now it seems there is another and this one is very interested in Stella.

Yes Stella is proving to be other than the rest of the magic beings and to find there is another like her or even greater than her in strength and magic terrified him. How could he protect her from someone with that kind of power? Neither he nor Stella had this particular gift.

George knew he had to bank his anger and fear for her sake. He held her close rocking her in his arms. All that mattered at this moment was the fact that she was once again safe and in his arms.

And now since they were both awake and adrenalin riding high, they turned their energies in a different direction and it didn't take long before sparks began to shoot out throughout the room.

What they brought to each other had everything leave their minds for a short time and only allowing all the pleasures they experienced and gave to each other to fill them. The panic left George while the fear left Stella now that they immersed themselves into what they received and gave to one another.

As they floated down onto the bed completely sated from their lovemaking, the sun peeked in through the window. Stella slid out of bed limp and limber. Shakily she made her way to the shower, leaving George to find his own way to re-hydrate.

When she finished she made her way toward the aroma of coffee dressed and ready for work. He was standing at the counter wearing only his suit pants. His torso was naked allowing her to gaze at his muscular chest. Even though they had just finished making love moments ago, lust built quickly in her again.

He watched her eyes glaze over and smiled. 'God,' he thought, 'there stands my miracle.' He walked over and put a cup in her hand as he leaned in and softly kissed her lips.

She wanted him right then and there and would have made a move toward her goal if someone wasn't knocking on the back door destroying the moment.

"I swear to God I'm going to start charging people for coming here. If they have to take a number and pay maybe they would think twice before coming."

She slammed her cup down on the table sending the coffee spilling over the rim slopping onto the table and stomped over to the steps leading down to the door. She knew her temper stemmed from her body going into lust overdrive but it didn't' help hearing George laugh as she went to answer the door.

Stella yanked the door open and was prepared to give the caller a good ripping when she saw it was young Stanley Hughes standing on the other side. Her irrational rage deflated like a pin-pricked balloon.

'Well hell,' she thought as she saw the look of trouble on his face.

Stanley saw the anger on her face before she banked it. "I'm really sorry for bothering you Miss Blake. My sister told me I shouldn't, but I just had to. It's really important."

The look on his face had her melting. She motioned him to follow her inside. She closed the door and led him up the steps to the kitchen.

"This kid looks like he could use a good shot of coffee," she tossed over her shoulder as she took him to the table and pushed him into a chair.

George complied setting a cup down in front of him then took his own seat. Stanley had come to see Stella, so he sat quietly sipping his coffee watching the nervous kid turning his cup around and around with shaky fingers.

"Okay Stanley, what's up?"

Stanley's head jerked up at the sound of her voice. He cleared his throat before speaking.

"Miss Blake, I know you're doing my sister a favour by looking into this matter for me. So first I want to thank you for that." He looked down at his coffee again unable to keep eye contact with her.

"It's alright Stanley, Naomi and I are friends as well as employee and employer. I'm happy to do it. Has something new come up?"

"Yeah, well, you told us not to have any physical contact with this Mr. Herrington, and we haven't."

"But? I can hear a but coming." She warned.

"Well here's the thing, Miss Blake. My lawyer received a letter from his lawyer asking for a meeting with all of us."

Stella's eyes narrowed at the ploy being played out. "That's really not a good idea. You tell your lawyer that you are unable to take the meeting and will do business with them only through your lawyers. Who's his lawyer?"

Stanley pulled out the letter from his lawyer reading through it until he came to the name. "Here it is. A Mr. Geoffrey Summerset," he read off.

Both George and Stella jumped up from the table scaring the whit's out of him.

"That son of a bitch! That sneaky low down son of a bitch!" Stella exploded.

"You will not meet with him." George ordered Stanley.

Stanley had spilled his coffee all over the table. He began stammering from the violent reaction from them both.

"Oh . . . okay . . . s . . . sure, no p . . .pro . . . problem. D . . . do you two know this lawyer?"

"We do yes. We most certainly do." George's eyes went to cobalt while Stella's were flashing green. "You must give us your word that you will not go to any meeting with them. Swear it."

His face had lost all of its colour now and he was visibly shaking from the sudden rage spewing out of the two of them. He knew they were holding something back from him, but by the look on their faces he really didn't want to know what it was. If this other lawyer could cause them to go off the handle like this, he was only too happy to comply.

"You have my word," he swallowed hard. "No meeting with them."

George recovered his composure faster than Stella. He stood by Stanley while Stella started pacing the room almost at a run.

"Stanley," George placed his hand on the boy's shoulder. "I'm sorry for the outburst. We know things about this lawyer that do not bode well for you and your sister and we are only thinking of what is in your best interest. I must insist though, that you keep your word and not meet up with him under any circumstances."

"Oh you don't have to worry. You scared any chance of that happening out of me." Stanley tried for a weak laugh to try and lighten the situation. "I'll keep my word."

"Stanley, your sister came to me for help and that is exactly what I'm trying to do for you both." Stella wanted to comfort the frightened young man.

"I do know that you are helping us and we can't thank you enough. But," he paused, "I just can't help feeling that there is more to this law suit that you two know and we don't." He shrugged.

"Your brains are showing through Stanley and yes there is more to it, but that is something we cannot divulge to either of you. Just do as we ask and things will work out, I promise. Trust me."

"Miss Blake, after the last time you helped us, I guarantee we do trust you. We will do everything you ask us to do." Stanley pinked up remembering the trouble he brought to his sister not that long ago.

"Stanley I can guarantee that this law suit will end in your favour. Your patent will hold up and the game and its name will be completely yours. But you need to listen to us and do as we ask. I will tell you that this so called lawyer is a very dangerous person and to keep you and your sister safe, you must never meet him in person."

"I promise we will do everything you ask us to do," Stanley assured her as he shook in his seat. "If you say don't meet him, we won't meet him."

Stanley got up and said his goodbyes to them. He didn't see the reaction his words had on Stella.

"That son-of-a-bitch won't touch him," Stella vowed after Stanley left the room.

"He won't, no," George agreed with her, his eyes narrowing as well.

Stella's brain went into overdrive to figure out what the hell Geoffrey was up to. This cat and mouse game with her family and the threats put upon young Stanley were increasing.

She knew this was all about trying to get his ring back. The fact that he was targeting humans and those humans were her friends told her he was getting desperate.

That really had her worried.

CHAPTER

Fifteen

George escorted young Stanley out while Stella continued her pacing. He could tell her rage was building and it was best if he got the boy out before she lost control and transformed in front of him.

He came back in and had to dodge the sparks shooting from her eyes. Taking a huge leap of faith, he made his way over to her and smart enough to place a shield over his hands before grasping her arms to stop her and to keep her in place. She turned her face to him and he had to dodge his head to avoid another spark.

"STELLA!" he yelled hoping to get through to her. "STELLA," he yelled again.

She stood quivering in his grasp. The red hot flames blazing in her eyes began to slowing fizzle away. She shook her head to clear it. The solid block of fear that settled over her took longer to melt away. Finally she was calm enough to let most of it slide off her and she looked at him with calmer green eyes.

George breathed a sigh of relief.

"I'm sorry George."

"It's alright Stella. I managed to get Stanley out before the fireworks began."

"How could I lose control like that?" she berated herself.

"Think about it Stella. Stanley comes in and drops a bombshell right after the nightmare that almost took you away. Anyone would lose control after that."

"That's an excuse, George. I should be stronger than that." She wouldn't forgive herself. She hated excuses. She never tolerated them from others and refused to seek one for herself.

"You are strong Stella and you're going to prove it by catching those two. When you do, we'll find a way to stop them for good." He hated when she doubted herself.

"George we can't kill them. That is against the rules. Killing them will affect both our worlds." Worry wouldn't leave her.

"No we can't kill them, but we will find a way to stop them. You don't have any archives to help you with your new powers, but I do. I'll go through them and maybe with what I find and your powers we'll find the way."

That brought some hope to her, lifting her spirits just a little.

"God George, I hope this will work." Stella told him. This is something she knew she has to rely on George to help her with.

Just hearing Stella agreeing to his help lifted his spirits and yes, his ego. Not being needed for his gifts has been such a hard blow to him that he felt lighter now and happier.

The next few days went without a hitch, unless of course, you didn't factor in the endless meetings at her mother's planning the wedding. That was just a smidgeon less threatening than being haunted by two Warlocks and a Wizard. At least the Manor was safely guarded so she didn't have to worry about her family.

Each time she went over, she had to put up with Tempest darting her looks of anger mixed with fear. It seems Tempest was blaming her for the trouble they were all in again. Gertrude was nervous but it didn't seem she shared her daughter's feelings of blame. The rest of the household were in their little happy zone swimming in the orchestrated plans for the wedding. God it was like they were all a bunch of event gurus. That gave her a shudder.

It didn't help either, that each time she left the Manor with a horrific headache from all the gushing and giggling over the wedding plans. Hen parties were simply not her thing. And it was times like these that she wished the whole wedding thing was over and done with.

As far as Stella was concerned she preferred to leave all the details to them and simply just show up in that wonderful gown Debra created for her.

Each time she thought about that wedding gown, she felt it against her skin and couldn't stop the smile remembering the sensation it gave her. She saw herself in it again and marveled at the beauty of it. It was like wearing the softest cloud in the sky. Stella knew there was nothing created by any designer that would come close to the absolute glorious vision of her wedding gown.

It was pure perfection and it was a true Debra Styles creation. The fact that she did design the perfect gown for her was another reason for her to love that energetic designer. Debra showed her that she knew exactly what is absolutely perfect for her. The gown showcased the perfect bodice. The entire gown was showcased in tier drop pearls. The billowing gatherings of the gown were also showcased in the pearls. The veil was secured by a tiara of sparkling jewels. This is a gown fit for any royalty in the World. The train was designed to fall gracefully behind the bride. It was gathered the same as the gown with tear-drop pearls to look like more clouds trailing behind her.

And because Debra was her friend and she was in her wedding party, the media would be there on her wedding day. Stella knew this dress was going to be the talk of the town, no, of the world, when it played in the news and was displayed in all the papers. This gown was the most beautiful thing that she felt that her friend has ever created.

She knew that Debra Styles was going to be an even bigger name in fashion designing once the world sees the dress, if that is at all possible. Once the world does see it she knew that Debra will be swamped with orders to create it for sales to other brides. That brought a huge smile to Stella's face. My God, but the gown she designed was so perfect in every way. Just knowing that she is the first one to wear this creation is such an honour. She felt ashamed that she didn't trust her to know that she would design the perfect wedding gown for her.

Stella's chest burst with pride for her friend and because of that she couldn't wait for the day of her wedding.

Just thinking of her friend brought back to her the first time they met. At first Stella was completely frustrated with this tiny pixie looking woman with a mind that couldn't hold a thought to save her life. Instead of describing the suspect's features, she kept harping on his clothes. It took a lot of time and patience for Stella to get and keep her on track. But once she did, she was amazed at all the details Debra was able to give to her.

It seemed that Debra took a huge liking to her even after all the grilling she went through. In Debra's mind Stella was so different from anyone she'd ever met. She kept insisting they go out for dinner and drinks once her case was over. For the first time in her life, Stella found that she simply could not shake off this scatter-brained little person. She finally ended up agreeing to go out with her thinking that will end her persistence. But after they did go out they became good friends. Friendship did not come easy to Stella and therefore she took that very seriously. It was due to her upbringing that she never felt she could trust others, but somehow this energetic person saw through her defenses and found a way to endear her to her. Stella thanked the powers that be that Debra cut through all Stella's earlier reserves and found a way to include her into her life.

Stella spent a lot of time searching for Elaine. Since she was alerted of her part in trying to trap her, she fell off the grid. She couldn't find her employed anywhere else since then.

Another thing bothered her as well. Since she somehow brought the other Warlock into her mind, there were no more sensations of being watched. Stella wondered if maybe this Warlock had moved on now. That was a large worry, not knowing if he would somehow come back and find a way to get at her now that she knew what he was.

Stella knew this was borrowing trouble with her hands filled with trouble already. But she couldn't help worrying about this strange Warlock and why he was so interested in her. She had to hope that she was strong enough to deal with him. According to her dreams she has to win or risk her family being destroyed.

The night of the opening for the musical 'Momma Mia' finally came. Elaine was still running around loose. George and Stella got dressed for the theater.

Dave had come through with the tickets but surprised her by showing her another pair of tickets. It seems that Louise and Dave were going with them.

That's not exactly how she had planned this. Now she had to worry about keeping them out of harm's way. It seemed lately that nothing was going to be easy for her.

It was a lot easier before Dave and Louise found each other. Before that, Dave would have scored her the tickets and left her to do her thing.

She frowned wondering how Louise managed to convince Dave to attend this musical. She knew he felt the same way about musicals as she did.

It really made her itchy watching him as he went around like a love sick puppy since he met up with the love of his life, things were bound to get a little messy once in awhile, like attending a musical she knew he didn't want to go to.

And she really didn't want the pair of them attending this one. But knowing Louise, she must have persuaded him to get a pair of tickets for them, once she heard he scored tickets for Stella and George.

Stella picked up her silver clutch purse that matched her flowing strapless silver gown, and placed her spare gun and cuffs in it when her phone rang. George, looking very suave and debonair in his tux glanced over lifting a brow.

She shrugged her shoulders and left the room to answer it.

"Hello?"

"Oh Stella," her mother's voice was excited on the other end. "You'll never guess who I just met."

"Mother, you're not supposed to leave the house." Stella panicked.

"Oh don't be silly dear, I didn't leave the house." Wanda giggled.

"Someone came to the house? Who?" Stella demanded.

"Yes someone came to the house dear. But I promised not to tell you who until you come here. It's so wonderful."

"Is everyone okay there?"

"Of course we are all okay. Would I be this happy if we weren't?" Wanda huffed.

Stella was torn. She wanted to rush to her mother's to see for herself that everything was alright and she needed to be at the theater hopefully to catch Elaine for Dave's sake.

George watched her biting her lip battling with herself. Finally unable to watch her struggling with her priorities any longer he walked over and took the phone from her. "Wanda is there an emergency there that needs Stella right away?"

"Of course not. I just told her we are all fine here." She snapped back wondering why these two didn't understand that.

"I'm sorry Ms. Blake. We were just heading out to the theater when you called."

"Oh, oh well of course you must go. Tell Stella I'll call her tomorrow then. I have some very good news for her. Enjoy your evening out."

"Thank you, we will. You have a pleasant evening too and we'll talk to you tomorrow." He hung up the phone.

He rubbed Stella's arm. "They are all well and safe. Apparently your mother has some good news for you. She'll call you tomorrow and we can both go over there together.

"Strange," Stella shook her head confused, but relieved that according to her mother there was no danger at the moment.

"Okay," she straightened her shoulders, "let's go catch a thief."

"It's always fun and games with you isn't it?" He laughed seeing the stress was gone for now.

They arranged to meet up with Dave and Louise in the parking lot. Louise thought that was silly as she and Dave would have been much more comfortable waiting in the lobby. She was tapping her foot by the time she saw them pull up and park beside Dave's car.

"I don't know why you wanted us to wait out here when the lobby would have been much more suitable and comfortable for us." She didn't hide her agitation as they climbed out of the car to join them.

"I'm sorry Louise, but I have a good reason for this. Would you mind if I have a private word with Dave before we go in?"

"Oh for heaven's sake Stella, you are going make us all late for the opening curtain." Her eyes narrowed.

"I know and I'm sorry but this is important." Stella didn't wait but grabbed Dave's arm and pulled him out of hearing distance from George and Louise.

When they were far enough away Dave yanked his arm free. "What is it Stella? I thought you wanted to see the show. Isn't that why you had me get the tickets?" Dave loved Louise and knowing her temper, he clearly didn't want to be on the receiving end of it.

"No I don't want to see the damned show. I hate musicals."

"But then why?"

"Because," she cut him off. "Elaine will be here. She loves them so much she won't be able to resist coming and I can take her here if she shows up. I need you to stick with Louise and keep her out of harm's way now that you've brought her here. I never asked you to get tickets for you and Louise.

"George is in on this too isn't he?" Dave shook his head slowly.

"Yeah, he's in on it. He's kind of like a backup for me. If I don't take her, he has some tricks up his sleeve that will do the job. All I need you to do now is to keep Louise safe, okay? I never asked you to bring her but now that you did I have to protect her."

Dave tipped his head back and gave out a short laugh. "Oh, I'll keep Louise safe, but I got to tell ya, I won't be able to keep the pair of you safe when she finds out she was being used." Now he let out a righteous laughter.

"I know for a fact that you can't stand musicals either, so what's the deal you getting tickets for you and Louise?" She cocked her head.

Dave had the good grace to bow his head and shuffle his feet. "Well I kind of mentioned that you wanted tickets for this show and Louise asked if I could get another pair of tickets for us."

"That's okay Dave, but from now on I think you should start screening your conversations with the love of your life or suffer enduring things you'd rather not," Stella smiled at his discomfort. "And another thing is that I didn't want her or you here tonight. Next time check in with me," she glared at him.

He knew she was right, but his back went up at being told that he was more a mouse than a man when it came to Louise.

"I may not enjoy the show inside, but then there is the after show when Louise finds out the real reason you wanted the tickets." He countered and a small grin spread over his face. After having Stella ream him out he felt justified in getting a bit of his own back at her.

"And that little show would not be brought about if you'd have kept your mouth shut," she seethed at him and was rewarded by seeing him cower.

'But yeah,' she thought, 'he's right about Louise's temper', making her cringe a little. They walked back to their partners and Dave led Louise through the parking lot to the theater, while Stella and George stayed behind to time their entrance for after the curtain raised.

Stella knew as they took their seats that Elaine wouldn't be stupid enough to sit in her box seat now that the police were looking for her. She'd blend in with the rest of the audience. Both George and Stella scanned the seats with their eyes while the rest of the people were staring at the stage.

A stroke of luck had Elaine and her boyfriend, Robert, sitting four rows down in aisle seats across the aisle from them. She was totally into the production being played on the stage, while Robert was fidgeting in his seat, clearly nervous. Stella never took her eyes off her for the entire first act.

The curtain began its descent. The house lights came on indicating the ending of the first act. Stella watched and waited as people got up to go to the lobby for refreshments and bathroom breaks. She stayed where she was and thought she had lost them when her view was blocked by the volume of people making their way out.

When the line of people thinned out she caught a glimpse of them remaining in their seats. She didn't think Elaine would run the risk of being recognized by anyone in the lobby. It was a good hunch and it paid off.

Since Dave sat next to Stella with Louise on his other side he knew the moment Stella spotted her quarry. He felt her tense up beside him. When most of the people had left he leaned over to whisper in her ear.

"Do you want me to take Louise out to the lobby?"

"Yeah, but try to stay out of Elaine's line of vision."

Dave stood up and offered his arm to Louise. She smiled up at him took his arm got up to walk out with him. She raised her eyebrows in question at the two still sitting.

"Aren't you two coming?"

"We'll join you in a bit Louise. I'd like to talk to George for a minute." Stella answered in a low voice.

"Fine," Louise's temper was beginning to simmer again. Something was off with these two. They were acting odd and spoiling what should have been a very lovely evening out. She decided that after the show she was going to have a few words with them.

Dave guided her out trying to keep them surrounded by the now thinning crowd heading out. He felt Louise tense up beside him and desperately hoped not to be in the fallout when she let her temper loose. He always considered himself a strong man, but when it came to Louise, well, it was run for cover, protect your ass and every man for himself. 'God help those two', he thought.

Looking around, she noticed there were only a handful of people that opted to remain in their seats. She really hoped that it would only be the four of them left. It couldn't be helped. She had to take her now.

Stella dug in her purse and pulled out her gun and a pair of handcuffs. The metallic sound of the handcuffs had Elaine's head snapping around. She locked eyes on Stella and jumped up. Elaine ran the other way with Stella hot on her heels. Her legs were longer and stronger than Elaine's and she was closing in on her fast.

Before Elaine reached the end of the row of seats Stella jumped on the next one using it as a spring board she leapt off of it and arrowed her body towards her. She dove at her catching her just before she reached the end of the row knocking her down between the rows of seats. Stella straddled her back yanking one of her arms behind her and slapped on the cuffs as she kicked her feet screaming out very inventive sexual self gratifications for Stella to use on herself.

When she looked up to search for George, she saw he had Robert in cuffs only a few feet from the exit. The few other people in the room were standing up. She'd heard one of the women scream when the chase started. They all stood silent now mouths open at the production they had just witnessed.

Stella let George call it in. They were walking their suspects out when the bell rang out ending the intermission. Timing was everything, she thought with a smile. But the smile didn't last. It faded fast as she caught the look on Louise's face when she passed her in the lobby.

'Oh crap,' she knew she was in for it when Louise got them alone. She looked over and saw George's shoulders droop. Well at least she won't have to suffer her temper alone.

The police arrived within minutes and relieved them of their charges. They escorted them out and Stella could hear one of the cops reading them their rights.

Looking at Dave's face and seeing the heavy guilt lifting from his shoulders just might be worth the tongue lashing that was coming in the near future.

Apparently the punishment was to start immediately. Stella's happy little thought of escaping the musical was thwarted by Louise's firm insistence that they go back into the theater and finish watching the production together. There was no getting around it. Stella, resigned to it, brushed her hands in her hair in an attempt to make it look half way decent.

As they made their way back to their seats, Stella whispered to George, "coward."

He only nodded his head. She snickered.

Stella could charge through a door, take down a drug induced criminal and even make suspects lose control over their bowels in interrogation, but she was every bit a coward like George, when it came to his foster sister.

Her shoulders drooped as they made their way back into the theater to watch the rest of the play. It didn't help matters to see the snide grin on Dave's face or catch the sound of subtle snickering from him.

Both she and George sat quietly during the rest of the show until it was over. They rose up to go following the crowd out of the theater. Neither one saying a word as they both slowly made their way out to the parking lot.

They knew that taking down the criminals inside was nothing compared to what they were about to face with a very angry Louise. All they could do was to brace themselves for what they knew for sure was coming their way.

They met up with them in the parking lot. The look on Louise's face was enough to stop a serial killer in his tracks. This is the part they both dreaded.

The look on Louise's face had Stella envisioning steam coming out of every pore of her. She vibrated where she stood with all the fierce anger building inside her.

Louise accused them of everything under the sun. Apparently she felt very strongly that they ruined a perfectly pleasant evening out.

According to Louise, neither one knew how to enjoy themselves and only thought of one thing, work.

She made it very clear to them that she was disgusted with them.

Stella stood there taking it all until she finally could take no more.

"Are you finished?" she asked her voice deceptively calm.

"You plan a perfectly wonderful night out and then proceed to ruin it by working," Louise challenged.

"Yes Louise, I planned to attend the show. I did not ask for you to join us. You butted in where you were not invited by getting Dave to get you tickets. You were not asked by me or George to accompany us to this theater production. My reason for attending was purely professional, whereas yours was to ingratiate yourself into my evening," Stella's eyes narrowed at her.

"The next time it might be wise to ask if we want your company when we make our plans." Stella stood toe to toe with her. "Apparently your only interest is to push your way in when not asked nor wanted.

"You never told Dave that you wanted to attend for purely work related reasons. I thought maybe we could all enjoy ourselves together." Louise countered and then spewed off for another ten minutes to her.

When she was finally finished with her tirade, Stella stared her down. "Do you always make it a habit to butt in where you are not wanted or asked to be? I do work for a living, whereas you do not. I earn my money where you just live on your own wealth. Next time I need David to do something for me, try asking me first before you just rush in and take over." Stella steamed back at her.

Although Louise gave them both a horrendous tongue lashing, she was stopped short of speech only for a moment after Stella said her piece to her. No one has ever spoken to her like this before. Even George knew not to displease her all the years they grew up together. Now this usurper in their lives was telling her that she has to check in with her before making plans. This woman, to her, was not suitable for her brother. She was going to watch every move of this Amazon woman and try to find something to convince her brother to get rid of her. But for now she was not going to let this woman get the better of her, no one ever has before. And Stella will definitely not be the first, she vowed to herself. Her brother deserves an elegant graceful woman of breeding to compliment his life and status.

CHAPTER

Sixteen

They were still nursing their bruised egos from Louise's vicious tongue lashing. She played over the scene of her waiting for them by their parked cars and letting into them as soon as they approached. Even Stella's attempts to put Louise in her place did nothing to stem her tongue. She kept them there and kept it up for a full twenty minutes longer not allowing anyone to interrupt her again. Stella swore she never heard her take a breath.

By the time she finished with them she'd accused them both of being workaholics to uncaring and unfeeling and never taking a moment or an evening off to simply enjoy the simple pleasures in life. According to Louise work was everything to them and placing their family and friends in danger meant nothing to them.

Stella sat on her sofa rubbing her ears. They were still ringing from it. "God, and to think Dave wants to tie himself permanently to that?" Stella's opinion of Dave went into question.

"Try living with that for years," George was rubbing his own ears.

"God, I don't know how you survived."

"Love, Stella, it has to be because I love her. She was really pissed this time."

"Jesus, I've never seen a person turn that colour of crimson or scream that long without stopping for air. I swear I saw steam coming off her. I think I've learned my lesson to never deceive her again."

"Well at least not until the next time," he laughed.

"We'll make the next time wait a long, long time." Now Stella joined in the laughter. "Now that's a woman with a weapon, God help Dave."

"Oh you didn't see his face. He was enjoying every minute of it watching her rip you a new one."

"Oh really, now that is interesting," she wiggle her eyebrows at him.

"Hmm, maybe I should have kept that bit of information to myself."

"George as much fun as you had, I will warn you now that I will not tolerate that behavior again. She is for all purposes your sister, but she will learn to never talk to me or treat me in that fashion again. If this is something you find you cannot live with, then you better tell me now." Stella's eyes narrowed. Just thinking of how Louise felt justified in her treatment of her made her angry again.

George knew she meant it. Suddenly he was put into the position of choosing between his beloved sister and the love of his life. It broke his heart to know that he simply cannot live without Stella and if that meant a rift between him and Louise, then so be it.

"I love and adore you my darling. I just hope that you and Louise can at some point come together. But if that is not to be, I must tell you again that I cannot live without you in my life." He told her with a heavy heart.

To hear the loyalty he has for her filled her. "I will try to get along with your sister, but I will not be treated like that again. I too love you and I sincerely hope that Louise and I can find some common ground. I know she has a good heart because she showed that to Debra. Let's hope that we can find a way to get on so you don't lose either of us." She patted his cheek.

They both went to bed on that hopeful note.

The smell of coffee woke her up the next morning. She stretched then yawning climbed out of bed. Donning her old battered robe and floppy slippers, Stella made her way to the kitchen.

George watched her shuffle in. Whether wrapped in expensive gowns and diamonds or an old battered robe and slippers, she was the most beautiful woman in the world to him. Love poured out of his eyes as he watched her take her seat at the table.

Stella took a sip and was blown back in her chair when she looked up to see the emotion streaming towards her from his eyes. Her heart fluttered like a humming bird's wings hovering at a flower sipping nectar. It took her breath away as her own powerful love welled up in her for him. All she wished at the moment was that this feeling would never lessen or go away ever over time. She desperately hoped that marriage won't change it. That was one of her secret fears about getting married.

George walked over to sit next to her. He ran his fingers softly down her cheek and watched her eyes glaze.

"You promised your mother you'd go over there today."

His words hit her like a splash of ice cold water instantly shutting off the hormones. She shook her head to get her balance.

"Well that killed any chance of me jumping your bones this morning," she frowned.

"I can't tell you how sorry I am for that, but we do have a problem that needs solving. Since it is still the weekend, I think we should take a little time for a visit before we settle back to it."

"Oh yea, a house full of estrogen, can't wait." She scowled. "I'd rather take on a Wizard and Warlock instead of that."

"Just remember you did some ass-kicking last night. Maybe that will hold you for a while." He smirked.

"The ass-kicking was great. The tongue lashing was hell," she reminded him.

"You got to love Louise's stamina," but he had the good grace to wince at the memory.

Stella pushed back in her chair. "Okay let me get dressed and then I want to write up the report for Mr. Yamada before we head over."

George knew it was her way of delaying the visit to her mother's. He let her get on with what she needed to do to get her mind prepared. While she was out of the room he rinsed their cups and did some thinking of his own.

They must have been watching for their arrival. As they climbed out of the car, Wanda and Maria stepped out onto the verandah to greet them. They were both sporting wide smiles.

Wanda was so excited she couldn't wait. She quick stepped it over to them putting an arm around her daughter and hurried her into the house.

Stella's brows winged up under her bangs at her mother's enthusiasm. She couldn't remember her mother being so excited before. Whoever this mystery caller is must be someone very special to her to have her so excited.

They were hustled into the house and shown into the parlor which was another strange thing in Stella's mind. The kitchen was always the room in this house for meetings and conversations.

Maria rolled up the tea cart in ceremonial style when they were all seated. Wanda acting the chatelaine began pouring tea for everyone. As soon as they all had their cups she sat back grinning like a cat, her eyes sparkling.

Stella couldn't take it any longer. The way her mother was acting was making her itchy. She set her cup down and leaned forward in her chair to look at her mother.

"Okay mother, spill it. You look like you're going to burst if you don't spit it out. Who is this person that came to visit and what is it about this person that makes you so excited?"

"Oh Stella," Wanda sat up so quick the tea in her cup was in danger of spilling over the rim. "He's back," she blurted out. "He's heard about your wedding and he came back for it." She giggled.

She was acting like a school girl. Stella had never seen her mother like this before. She watched her preening her hair, eyes glowing and smiling so wide it hurt Stella's face just watching it.

"Let me repeat, who is this person?"

"Well, your father of course." Wanda couldn't help giggling again.

Stella almost fell out of her chair. George was instantly on his feet and by her side resting his hand on her shoulder in support. She managed to look up at him with wide stunned eyes and saw instant alarm in his.

"Isn't it wonderful?" Wanda's excitement blinded her from her daughter's reaction. "He wants to know if you would let him have the honour of giving you away."

"Father . . . give . . . me away," Stella managed between gulps of air she tried to force in and out of her lungs.

While Stella's mind fought hard to digest this information, something clicked in George's. He turned to Wanda searing her with a cold look.

"How long has he been here?" Realizing a Warlock had been in the area undetected by him filled him with a combination of fear and rage. How could it be that he never sensed this Warlock? This is unheard of. If this Warlock possesses the power to block detection from other Warlocks, Stella could be in a great deal of danger.

"Garrett said he'd only been in town for a few weeks." She blushed. "He said he was working up the courage to visit us. He can be so sweet that way, you know."

"NO, WE DON'T." George's rage was consuming him now.

Wanda's head snapped up at the sharp tone in his voice. Her cup fell to the floor spilling tea over the rug. She clasped her hands to her chest. Fear filled her at the sight of his cobalt eyes filling with hot blinding rage. She gasped at the fire burning behind them.

Maria was by her side in a second with her wand held out towards him. She knew his magical powers couldn't work in the house, but that didn't mean he couldn't physically harm her friend. He had the look of murder in his eyes.

Stella was still too stunned to take in the scene playing out in front of her. She was shocked to the core. Never in her lifetime had her mother ever mentioned her father before. He was never in her thoughts all the time she was growing up. That was just the way it was. Now this Garrett person was thrown at her and she didn't know what to do about it or how to handle it.

"Back away Warlock," Maria spat at him. "Back away or suffer the consequences," backing up her threat by waving her wand at him.

Somewhere behind the rage, Maria's words got through and he did step back but kept his flaring raging eyes on Wanda.

Gwen rushed in the room hearing the raised voices and stopped dead. The look of terror on her mother, the stunned look of her sister, the rage from both George and Maria had her in a conundrum of who to go to. She decided to fill the room with waves of calm hoping to ease everyone's tensions. She watched as her mother began to breathe easier and her sister began to relax, but the tension between Witch and Warlock were too strong to be affected by it.

Wanda recovered enough to speak.

"What is wrong with you George? I give you both good news and you act like I've committed some crime." The stress had chased away all her joy.

"Good news? You call it good news that another Warlock has been in this area and I have not sensed him? That should not be. Every Warlock senses another in the same area. Do you know what kind of danger this brings to Stella?"

George was beyond rage, his entire body filled with a burning inferno.

Gwen's calming wave brought Stella around. She could feel the heat emitting from him and knew he was in danger of burning up from the inside because the house wouldn't allow it to escape. She knew what she had to do. She had to get him out of the house before he imploded.

She jumped up and with all the strength she possessed, she pushed and pushed him until she shoved him out the door. The moment his feet touched the verandah the fire exploded from him. The wave of heat bursting from him blew her off her feet sending her to land face down on the driveway.

She got up scraped and bruised from the stones and knew she had to act fast or the house would burn down. She drew the heat into her and felt herself rise up. She lifted her arms and invited the wind that circled her loosening her hair to fly around her head.

Her eyes sparked as she threw a shield around him to encompass the flames around him. She called to the earth and it rumbled beneath him knocking him off balance. She called to the wind to carry him from the house and set him down on the lawn.

She called to him in a voice so sweet and gentle. "George, let go. You must let go now. I need you to let go of the rage and let my love in."

As she kept pleading with him, she saw the fires around him lessen in strength until finally they were gone. She released the heat and gently floated down. As soon as her feet touched ground she raced over to him knelt down and cradled him in her arms.

The danger was over.

Stella was not prepared to let his powers be taken away again. Not when that was a risk to his life. She called to her family to come outside. Now that the rage was gone from him, she knew they could talk about this new development calmer, but outside the Manor.

It took a bit of doing but between Stella and Gwen they convinced Wanda and Maria they would be perfectly safe. Maria grudgingly brought out another tea tray and they sat on the verandah to discuss this new development. Stella noticed that Maria wasn't willing to put her wand away though.

"Put that stick away Witch or suffer the consequences. You will not threaten the love of my life," Stella screamed over at Maria and watched her stumble from this verbal attack on her from her little one.

"He was about to hurt my friend and your mother," Maria finally managed to get out.

"My mother has brought danger to us. George was trying to protect us." Stella countered. "You interfere with our protection again Maria and you will be banished from our sight." Stella glared at her.

The threat of that had Maria almost buckle and fall. This woman she raised and tended to all through the years, now turning on her was beyond anything she could imagine. This Warlock that her friend found so amorous and amusing must be a great threat to this family.

Of course she was there when the two of them came together, but she didn't sense anything different until he left. That was when she saw a very big change come over her friend. Having Stella showing such adversity against him must be a sign that this Warlock was a true danger.

Wanda's eyes went wide from the accusations. She thought they would be as overjoyed as she was. How could she have known they would have this reaction to what she felt was wonderful news?

Stella turned to George.

"George do you feel you can explain to us this concern you have without getting angry?" She sent angry eyes at her mother pinning her where she sat.

Once he'd recovered he felt ashamed of his reaction that endangered their lives and his. He apologized profusely to them. Knowing the danger Stella had been placed in was no excuse for what almost happened here. It was because of his all consuming love for her that he reacted the way he did. But knowing that his actions almost had her living without him had him making the effort to keep his emotions under control.

"Yes, darling, and I'm sorry for what I put you all through. I hope you can forgive me Ms. Blake."

"Of course George," Wanda still didn't understand why her good news was met with such violent reactions from them both.

Stella still in protective mode over George kept sending scathing looks to her mother.

"I will deal with you later," Stella seethed out at her mother.

"First I must repeat that this has never happened as far as I know. Never has a Warlock been in the same area as another and not been sensed by the other. This Warlock has other gifts than the rest of us and that gave me great cause to worry.

"Stella has had the feeling of being watched for a few weeks now. We determined it wasn't from any human but by magic. I'm convinced that this Garrett is the one who has been watching her."

Stella told them of her trip to the park and described the man she saw in her mind. She watched her mother smile nod her head indicating that it was indeed Garrett she saw.

Seeing what this caused George, she raised her hand and had her mother flying off the veranda and onto the front lawn. She went over to her mother and stood over her with fire in her eyes.

"How dare you put us in this danger," she seethed. "You have always been a silly woman and now you put us in great danger. I should banish you from here." Stella raged at her.

Wanda sat where she landed looking up at her daughter. She'd never seen such anger from her before and it frightened her. Never before has she ever shown violence towards her. Her daughter has changed so much she barely recognized her now.

"Stella dear, he is not here to harm any of us. He would never do that," she pleaded.

"Mother, why would the Warlock that sired me want to come back and be part of the wedding? I thought that once the mating was a success the Warlock and Elfin blood parted ways, never to have contact again. This is a dangerous man, a danger to us all," she spat out.

Wanda's head snapped up at the tone of her voice. "Oh that's very true darling. I do not expect to ever see Gwen's father. All I can say is that Garrett is very different and wonderful." A dreamy look came over her. "Darling he is not dangerous."

"So you say," Stella was still filled with anger at her mother.

"Well I think we can all agree that this Warlock is very different," Gwen asserted.

"Yes," George agreed. "And I don't think we can rule out dangerous."

Wanda, seeing the anger still in her daughter's eyes, got up and timidly walked back to the veranda. She brushed herself off and steeled herself to appear strong.

"Oh nonsense George," Wanda dismissed his concerns. "I told him I would arrange for you to meet him Stella."

George tried to jump out of his chair but Stella took a firm grasp on his arm to keep him where he was. She was just as concerned but they needed to talk this out to seek answers.

"George, do you think he will be under the same restrictions as you inside the Manor?" She asked softly.

He took a deep breath to regain his composure. "I can't be sure. It seems he not only has the same powers as me but he also has different ones. If he can get around the Manor's shield we need to find a way to protect everyone."

"I'm telling you right now, the two of you are worrying unnecessarily. He would never hurt Stella." Wanda frowned at them both.

"Ms. Blake, when it comes to Stella's safety I will not be careless."

Wanda could not question the depth of love he has for her daughter. But she knew Garrett and they didn't. She knew Garrett would never harm his own daughter. He was different from her other mate. He gave of himself.

It was a true bonding of spirit and soul. Even after he left she couldn't bring herself to be with another. He touched her heart and filled it with so much love for him. That was something that did not happen to mates of Elfin and Warlock blood.

"Mother," Gwen has thought of a solution. "To put George's mind at ease, why don't we meet with this Garrett somewhere where George retains his powers so he feels better able to help Stella if it becomes necessary?"

"But I'm telling you all that Stella is in no danger from him."

"Yes, but they don't know him like you do and this will have everyone feeling more comfortable."

"Oh for heaven's sakes, fine then. Where do you suggest we all meet?" Wanda was annoyed with them all.

"How does the clearing behind the woods sound to everyone?" Gwen suggested.

They all agreed and Stella and George left the Manor leaving Wanda in charge of setting up the meeting with Garrett Stone.

Stella remained concerned. Her mother, because of her gifts ruined her first choice of careers. Would this Garrett person ruin the career she now has?

She glared at her mother for her lost dreams and was determined that no one, not even this long lost father would ruin this career she has. She had carried this resentment towards her mother for a long time now. Yes, she loves her mother, but she lost everything that made her happy. No way was she going to allow anyone, not even her mother, this stranger or George to lose what she has now. Stella knew that losing this career she has now would be the end of her.

"I will not have you or anyone ruin the career I have now like you did to my Police career," Stella warned her mother and watched her snap back at that statement. "You destroyed my career and hopes and dreams and I will not allow you or this mate of yours to do that to me again." She stated so firmly it shocked everyone.

It took some time for her to come around after that accusation was thrown in her face. She never realized it was because of her that Stella left the force. At the time she thought that she was helping her.

Guilt filled her now to realize that it was her careless words that ended Stella's wonderful career. She sat taking time to think it all through and only wished she knew how to make it up to her.

At the time she knew her daughter was still in denial about what flowed in her blood. Her only thought was to help her, but it seems doing that was the worst thing she could have done at that time. Taking what her daughter treasured most away from her deeply troubled her. To know it was her that lost her daughter's dreams and position on the Force was very hard to face.

Now that she found the Warlock that captured her heart all those years ago and to know he wished to renew their relationship was so joyful for her. She hoped deep down that Stella will see that he means no harm to her.

Wanda went around dreamy-eyed just thinking of seeing and talking to Garrett again. While Maria went about with a different attitude, she was not so convinced that this Warlock is as good as her friend tells herself. Plus the fact, that her little darling had turned on her and threatened her. This told her that Stella was under a great deal of pressure right now. She needs to protect her little one.

Maria was determined to stay close to Wanda and ready to step in should she have to. Yes she was there when this Warlock came into her life, but that brought the thoughts back that even then she didn't trust him.

It surprised them all to see anger building up behind Stella's eyes. And for the first time in her life, she spoke her true feelings to them all. "Whatever comes of this meeting, I will not have this Warlock destroy what I have built for myself, like you did to my career on the Force mother." She raged.

Wanda's surprise at her daughter's statement took her aback. But even the tears that it brought to her did not soften Stella's heart at the moment. Her mother was to blame for her resigning from the Force and that was a pain still kept deep inside her. That was a hurt she didn't think would ever heal. She always felt betrayed by her mother after what she did that day.

Leaving the Force was the hardest thing she ever had to face and she vowed to herself right then and there that no one would ever take away from her what she felt deep down she was destined to do. Law was in her blood and whatever happens she knew deep down that she has to be part of that. Seeing criminals caught and brought to justice was so much a part of her that she didn't feel she could go on or live without being part of that process either on the Force or in her new career as a Private Investigator. Because of the way she felt she will never allow anyone ever to take this away from her again.

This was the first time Stella announced to them the reason for her leaving the job she worked so hard to achieve and keep. Her mother's tears did nothing to placate her feelings on what she did to her.

To Stella, all her hard work was for nothing when her mother stepped into her meeting that day telling all her men that she saw and spoke to spooks and ruined all the hard work she put in to get to the position she so desperately wanted. Her mother ruined her career and was the reason for her quitting the Force. She vowed she would not allow her to ever take anything more away from her. She could still see the shock on all her men's faces after Wanda finished talking. Those few simple words she spewed out lost all the respect her squad had for her. Without their respect she could not lead them anymore. She knew her superiors would also take a dim view of her once they got wind of the rumours. She had no choice but to resign her position as Lieutenant of the Homicide Division.

To Stella, her mother just ruined her entire career with a few misguided words. Her mother lost her the career she worked so hard to achieve. For this she can never forgive her.

This is the first time that Wanda realized what she did to her daughter. She thought that at that time she was simply trying to help. Never did she ever think that her words would cause her daughter to lose what she worked so hard to achieve. She never knew that it was that day and her words that caused her daughter to leave the job and career that meant so much to her.

CHAPTER

Seventeen

G eorge tried to make up to Stella for his behavior at her mother's house by taking her out to dinner. He called the Belvedere and booked a table for them at their best restaurant in the building, Chez Francois.

Listening to her state the reason for her leaving the job she worked so hard to achieve and place the blame for it where it truly belonged must have been the hardest thing she had ever done up until now. He did realize that she kept this to herself not wanting to hurt her mother, but after hearing her spew it all out he realized the mental damage her mother caused her. Now all he wanted was to try to give her some peace and time to fully resolve her feelings about it. George had no idea until now the damage her mother caused her back then. Things became a little clearer for him now. Now all he wants is to be there for her and support her.

They had plenty of time to relax before making their reservation. It wasn't for hours yet so George decided to treat Stella to a drive in the country to take in the quiet and give them some time for them to be alone together.

But as everyone knows the best laid plans usually end up with a hitch. They were about to climb into George's car when Stella's cell rang. She shrugged her shoulders took it out of her pocket and answered it.

"Stella, I'm so sorry to bother you," Naomi's voice sounded edgy.

"No problem Naomi. What is it? If it's a battle between the lawyers I'm afraid I can't be of much use."

"No, no, yes, but no," she stammered.

"Naomi, calm down. Take a deep breath and calm down and tell me what's wrong."

Naomi did as Stella asked and she heard her take a big breath and blow it out before starting again. It helped.

"We were supposed to go to our lawyer's. But Stanley got a call before we could head out and he took off. Stella I can't find him. He isn't answering his cell phone. I'm so worried Stella." Naomi began to weep openly now.

"Who was the call from?" Ignoring the crying on the other end, her tingle went into overdrive.

"I don't know. He put the phone down and ran out of the house. He wouldn't even answer me when I called after him. He got in the car and drove off. Oh, Stella, I'm so worried."

"Are you at home now?"

"Yes."

"Stay there and we will be there in a few minutes." Stella ended the call putting her phone back in her pocket and not looking at George, they climbed in the car and headed straight for Naomi's.

George drove as fast as he could. Stella only asked him one question on the way.

"Do you sense him?"

"No," he answered not taking his eyes off the road.

Stella knew that meant that Geoffrey was not in the area telling her the son was the one that called Stanley and probably has him now. This was their way of getting George and Stella to go after them.

The car squealed to a halt in front of Naomi's home. She was waiting at the open door by the time they reached it. She showed them in to her small parlor on shaky legs. George went to get the wine to help settle her down. He came back in the room with it to see Stella cradling the poor little thing as tears washed down her face.

After a few sips she managed to sit up on her own, her hands a bit steadier.

"George can you check to see who the last caller was?"

While he went to do that, Stella took out her notebook and began to question her accountant.

The call came in a couple of hours ago. No she had no idea who it was. No, Stanley didn't say anything to her. She'd called his friends and they hadn't heard from him. He took off down the street heading east.

"Private number," George said to Stella when he came back. "I've got the phone company checking the call now."

Stella knew there wasn't much more she could do. She told Naomi to stay in the house and not answer the phone or the door until she got back to her. Her only lead was the direction Stanley headed.

It looked like the dinner was off and the road trip was back on. They had to risk it if they were to find Stanley. They headed back to her office to find the map she had charted with what she deemed were the most probable locations for the two rogues.

They hunkered down over the map. Both of them giving their input on what they thought should be the first places to check. Satisfied with their choices Stella folded the map stuffed it in her pouch and headed for the door.

Just as George reached for the doorknob to open the door, Stella put on the brakes. An idea flashed in her mind stopping her in her tracks. George looked at her cocking an eyebrow at her hesitation. The look on her face told him her uncanny instinct was giving her an idea. He let go of the doorknob and waited enthralled at the process going on in her head.

Finally impatient, "Stella what is it?"

"He's not here," she frowned still formulating the idea that came to her.

"No, he is not here. I don't sense him. I told you that."

"Right," she suddenly looked up at him with clear green eyes. "He's not here. But what if he wants to be here, he'd have to get you out of the area to do that."

George thought a minute and then it became clear where her mind was going.

"So, if we started searching outside the area, he could slip in. Yes that makes sense. He must have Wilfred watching us to see what we are doing."

"Yeah, I think so too. Hang on. I need to make a call." She pulled her cell out.

Twenty minutes later they pulled up in front of Dave Palmer's Security. They walked in. As soon as Stella saw Dave, she apologized for hauling him in on the weekend and possibly spoiling plans he and Louise might have had.

Their meeting lasted for a little over half an hour while they got everything in place. Two people resembling them wearing their clothes and the woman wearing a long red wig tied back walked out and climbed into George's car and headed east. Dave sat with George and Stella awhile before they left wearing the imposter's clothes climbed into a borrowed car with tinted windows. They headed out to drive around the city.

They drove around for a couple of hours when George got the first sense and zeroed in on it. He pushed his foot down on the accelerator and made a bee-line to the location.

Geoffrey knew the moment he was sensed. He almost missed it, it was so weak. Without his ring all his powers were dimmed. His face showed shock at first and then filled with rage at being out-smarted. He was so sure they'd leave the city to find that little gamer wimp.

It didn't help that his son had told him that he watched the Warlock and his Elfin bitch leave from the security guy's place and headed east out of the city. He knew he wouldn't be able to shake off the Warlock now that he got a sense of him.

Driving fast he reached for his cell and called his son. He knew there was no getting around it. He'd have to make a stand and deal with him, but he won't be alone for that, he'd have his son helping him.

"Let's see him take on a Warlock and a Wizard," his grin was feral as he gave the directions to his son to meet him there.

It didn't take George long to figure out where Geoffrey was headed when they neared the street to the Blake Manor. Seeing the direction George was going had Stella realize where they were going to end up. She tried to keep her seat as George took corners on two wheels. She reached for her cell and called her sister.

After a short conversation with her she outlined a plan that would have Gwen present for the battle. The women at the Manor were all prepared and ready when George pulled up at the foot of the steps.

They stepped out of the car. "Oh God, not now," Stella shook her head as the hairs on the back of her neck stood up.

George whipped his head around when she spoke. "What is it Stella?"

"Garrett, he's watching me. I don't need this distraction."

"You said when you concentrated and saw him, he stopped. Try that now. Take a few minutes and try."

"Yeah," Stella closed her eyes concentrating, searching for him. His face came to her almost taking her breath away at his beauty. He was smiling and then suddenly a frown appeared on his face and he was gone. The sensation was gone as well.

"Okay, it worked," she breathed a sigh of relief. She looked at her mother with awe at the strength it must have taken to let him go.

But her fears of what this Garrett could do to her new career had that feeling banked pretty quickly.

Her mother knew the moment her daughter saw his face. She was smiling at her now.

Stella saw the look on her mother's face and scowled at her.

"This is not the time for that mother." She seared her mother with a vicious look. "Think what you might, but I will brook no interference from this stranger." She spat. "I will deal with you later."

That wiped the smile off her mother's face.

George rubbed Stella's arm to calm her down. They needed to keep focused on the business at hand. He just hoped that this unknown Warlock would hold off whatever he has in mind long enough for them to deal with Geoffrey and his son.

"Okay now, if everyone is ready we better go." George took the lead. The rest of them all followed closely behind him.

George placed a shield around them as they hurried towards the woods.

Wanda's happiness simmered away from the look from her daughter and the words she flung at her. She just couldn't understand why Stella felt such animosity to her.

She remembered how she accused her of ruining her job on the Force and that too she didn't understand. But the truth of the pain was clearly on her face and in her words and it did hurt.

Now that she knew Stella saw Garrett, Wanda could not understand why she was still so angry. She'd told her she had good news for her. But Stella's attitude kept telling her she only wanted to battle Garrett. Somehow she had to convince her daughter there was no need for that.

Wanda just hoped that after this business was done, that she could sit her daughter down and explain everything to her. Surely she'd understand once she heard all of the facts.

Maria noticed Wanda's mind wandering and gave her a little nudge, before taking up her position, to get her back to the serious business at hand. She was not of the same mind set as Wanda. If this Warlock was watching her precious girl and scaring her, then she too did not trust him and she felt she has to protect Stella no matter what the cost to her and her friendship with Wanda.

CHAPTER

Eighteen

They made their way slowly towards the woods. The closer they got, the stronger George could sense Geoffrey. No one said a word as they made their way, each one busy mentally preparing themselves for an attack.

Gwen stayed in the rear with her mother. Her job was to use her calming waves if needed and to protect her mother. Morgana was ahead of them to deflect any flying objects. Gertrude, Tempest and Maria walked directly behind George and Stella with their wands out ready and raised high to use in a moment's notice. The one thing that worried them was the fact that all Witches have to obey a Warlock. Maria felt she will be forced to obey the Warlock of her choice. She didn't know if her dear friend Gertrude and her daughter will agree with her choice.

They reached the woods looking very much like an army. The first attack came in the form of a fireball aimed directly at them.

George countered it with one of his own. The three Witches sent out a stream of lightning bolts that fell just short of their mark.

Geoffrey and Wilfred had shields up for their protection.

The blast from the Witches only fuelled Geoffrey's rage. He hadn't counted on the Warlock and Elf-blood to bring backup, especially from Witches. The Witches didn't bother him since they were low on the chain of power. He knew the history and knew that Witches must obey a Warlock.

Knowing his powers were weaker without his ring only enraged him more now that he knew they were outnumbered. It was his rage and massive ego that kept him from retreating.

Wilfred, having dealt with George before was sure he could out-smart him at his tricks. Neither father nor son was willing to give an inch. Both felt together they were a strong enough force to bring down the Warlock that stole the ring. The rest were only Elfin and Fairy blood and Witches. They were no more than ants to be squashed.

The clearing was coming up fast. Stella touched George's arm to stop him before they reached it. He turned to look at her. Stella concentrated on bringing the heat inside her. As it built a wind began to slowly swirl around her lifting her up. The band holding her hair back flew off and her hair blew out around her head and face in a fiery halo. Her sea-green eyes sparked as she rose.

She lifted her arms out building a shield to encompass those behind her.

With one arm she indicated they proceed. She began to grow and grow until she was a formidable sight. She cast her fiery-lit eyes to the skies and watched as white clouds appeared and begin to build and swarm the sky.

Just as they were about to step out of the woods into the clearing, the clouds turned dark. Lightning flashed down searing the ground a few feet from Geoffrey and Wilfred.

George halted and looked up at Stella only to see confusion cross her face. He knew at once that another force was responsible for the change. His eyes turned to cobalt steel as his rage took over thinking she was in great danger.

With all the power that he possessed he threw out his shield in an attempt to protect her. It met her shield and sizzled. Fear had sweat pouring out of him as he tried again and again to protect her.

Suddenly George was sent hurdling back into the woods. Stella searched for the source almost releasing the heat in the fear that he was harmed. Then ripe anger took over her filling her with so much rage.

She began to grow and grow as her powers grew. She now towered over the trees around them. Thinking that somehow Geoffrey had developed a new power that could destroy her love, she floated toward them. Flashes of blazing fire shot from her eyes at the two standing yards away from her.

All she wanted at this time was to destroy the two. She raised her hands and called for the sun. Burning pieces of fire fell down from the heavens to land in her hands. The winds around her nearly knocked the two off their feet.

"YOU DARE TO HARM MY LOVE!" Her voice boomed out echoing through the clearing almost deafening them. She stood towering over them now ready to kill.

Wanting to kill them. Everything in her wanted them to burn in hell.

She cast out a wave of hot sizzling air ripping across the clearing this time blasting them off their feet. Geoffrey was so shocked to find his shield did nothing to block it.

She drew back her hands ready to cast the burning balls in her hands at them when suddenly another being as large as she floated in the clearing.

"STELLA YOU MUST NOT DO THIS." His voice boomed out the warning causing more shock waves sending all the others scrambling to keep their footings.

Shocked at the sight of another with her powers, she turned to stare at him.

"HOW DARE YOU INTERFERE? WHO ARE YOU TO TELL ME WHAT TO DO?" Her fear for George seared the rage consuming her now leaving no room for rational thinking.

"I AM GARRETT, YOU'R FATHER. PLEASE CHILD YOU MUST LISTEN TO ME. YOU MUST NOT DESTROY THESE TWO. DESTROYING THEM WILL DAMAGE ALL OUR WORLDS."

"I KNOW YOU HAVE BEEN WATCHING AND FOLLOWING ME. IF IT IS A BATTLE YOU WANT WITH ME, THEN A BATTLE YOU WILL GET." She turned her fiery eyes on him drawing back the hand holding the piece of sun to whip it at him.

Geoffrey and Wilfred sat stunned, frozen at the sight of these two powerful beings. Nothing in their archives or history prepared them for such beings. They had never come up against anything as powerful as these two gargantuan beings.

Her family stood shaking just inside the woods watching the confrontation. They thought that only Stella possessed such powers and to see another and seeing her willing to do battle had them terrified for her.

The wind created from the two bowed the trees around them making it difficult for them to remain on their feet. The sky was dark and heavy with swirling clouds. Lightning flashing all around them had them afraid this might be the end.

Morgana was using all her mental strength to keep flying debris from hitting them. The Witches gathered close together ready with their wands to thwart off chants or spells that could make their way towards them. George was back on his feet and try as he might he could not get close to Stella to help her.

Garrett raised his hands chanting words restraining her efforts to hurl the molten ball at him.

"I AM NOT HERE TO BATTLE WITH YOU MY DAUGHTER BUT TO STAND WITH YOU." Garrett drew nearer to her.

"STAND WITH ME? YOU, WHO SNUCK AROUND SPYING ON ME, NOT EVEN MAN ENOUGH TO APPROACH ME FACE TO FACE! I DON'T NEED A COWARD TO STAND WITH ME. RELEASE YOUR HOLD SO I CAN DESTROY THOSE TWO MURDERING BASTARDS," Stella demanded still in full rage.

"WE WILL TALK ABOUT YOUR ACCUSATIONS LATER," Garrett boomed out. His face flinched with her hurtful remarks.

Stella couldn't trust him, wouldn't trust him. Not yet anyway. She needed to deal with the two that wished harm to her love. She darted her blazing eyes back and forth from Geoffrey and his son to the man calling himself her father. As she floated above considering how best to deal with the one problem and keeping her eyes on the other, it gave Geoffrey just enough time to pull himself together.

Glimpsing George's figure standing just inside the woods behind her and to the side, he gestured to his son and they launched another attack on him. George's shield was down and they hit their mark sending him flying in the air hurtling him back into the woods.

Thinking him hurt, or worse, dead, the pain seared through her heart. She felt this entity caused her to lose focus. She screamed shaking the ground around them releasing Garrett's invisible hold on her. She lifted her hands ready to cast the balls of sun at them to incinerate them where they stood. They will not live, she vowed to herself.

Just as she was ready to release the ball, she found her hands wrapped in a golden rope this time. She went wild with fury screaming at this being who dared to stop her. The earth rumbled, the trees shook violently, uprooting the closest ones. The wind grew to almost hurricane strength in her fury.

Garrett created another golden rope to bind Geoffrey and his son before rushing over to his daughter.

"I WILL KILL YOU," The earth beneath them cracked at her screams.

"NO, STELLA, YOU WILL NOT AND YOU WILL NOT KILL THESE TWO EITHER. I WARNED YOU OF THE CONSEQUENSES SHOULD THAT HAPPEN." He came over to her. "THE TWO ARE BOUND NOW. LET GO OF THE HEAT AND WE WILL TALK. PLEASE DAUGHTER, LET GO OF THE HEAT." He pleaded, stroking her hair gently as she frantically struggled to get loose.

"You dare touch me when those two have killed my love?" she screamed at this stranger.

Her attempts at freeing herself were no good. She couldn't loosen the binding on her. She was frantic with worry not knowing if George was lying dead or hurt. If he was lying to her, she just put all her family and friends in mortal peril. Her mind saw her family as they appeared in her dream, all lying dead around her. Tears spilled down her cheeks at the thought. And she went wild.

"I WILL NOT ALLOW YOU TO HARM MY FAMILY. FIGHT ME, FIGHT ME AND LEAVE MY FAMILY BE. I AM THE ONE YOU WANT. I WILL DESTROY YOU. RELEASE THESE BINDINGS NOW OR SUFFER THE CONSEQUENCES." Stella raged.

Screaming at him that he killed her family, she cast out threats at this usurper and struggling harder had her grow to monumental size.

The vibrations from her booming screams had more trees uprooted and flying around them.

Garrett grew with her fearing for her safety. He forced himself to grow with her in order to keep his hold on her. If she did not calm down, she might die from her own rage.

As hard as she tried she could not free herself. Finally she realized she had no choice it seemed. Still filled with anger, she released the heat and began to float down to the ground. The winds died down. Once she was lying on the ground her family rushed to her circling her. The blast George took from those two had not killed him but blew him ten feet back into the woods. He was scraped and bruised, a little singed but alive.

On shaky legs he made his way back out to help her. When he reached the clearing again he found her transformed back and lying helplessly on the ground with her family hovering around her.

"Oh God, I've destroyed my family," she wept.

Garrett floated down and stood before them. Wanda surprised them all by running to him and wrapping her arms around him. She wept on him.

Even in her weakened state, Stella watched with fearful eyes as he gently cradle her mother in his arms like a lover.

In that moment she felt two things, disgust for her mother's weakness and betrayal and hate for the man who bound her and kept her from protecting her family.

Running to this man, her mother put the whole family at his mercy. Her mother betrayed her own family.

George made his way over on shaky legs. He knelt down beside Stella taking her in his arms, all the time keeping his eyes on Garrett, Geoffrey and Wilfred. It appeared the golden rope prevented them from using their powers. He knew his powers would do nothing against this stranger and it made him very uneasy and angry to be useless to the love of his life.

He held her close thinking if she was to die, he would die with her. If what she screamed was true, then he wished to die with her. He lifted rage filled eyes at this stranger knowing he was incapable of battling him and winning.

George prepared himself for death clinging to his beloved.

Garrett looked down at his daughter. His chest filled with pride. He calmly walked over still holding Wanda near him. He kissed the top of her head before gently releasing her.

"You are everything I could have hoped for in a daughter, Stella. I am so proud of you." He released the golden rope from her wrists.

When her breathing came more natural, she looked up at him. His words shocked her.

"You have been stalking me, watching me. Why?" She wasn't ready to trust him yet. "If you are here to do my family harm, then let me warn you, you will have to go through me first and I won't be so easy to kill now that I know some of your tricks."

"Stella, I'm not here to harm you any of you, I promise."

"Easy words," she spat back at him.

"George take me out of here. Mother is a traitor and this man wants to kill my family." She screamed at George.

George was on the verge of transporting her out with him when Garrett spoke.

"I am sorry if I gave you cause for alarm. You see, your mother and I had something extraordinarily special and I wished to see her again and what we produced. Then I heard of your upcoming wedding and wanted very much to be a part of that."

Stella pondered on that answer for a minute. She still didn't understand what made his union with her mother different than her sister's. Mentioning her mother brought the fact of her betrayal to them all flying back in her face.

"Warlocks and Elf blood are not known for any attachment after the mating is a success. What makes you so different?" She needed answers not willing to let go of her suspicions and anger yet. She stalled for time until her strength came back so she could fight him.

Garrett bent his head back and laughed long and loud.

"And you mother, you are a traitor to us all," she spat at Wanda.

She watched her mother flinch at her hurtful words. Sensing her pain, Garrett wrapped an arm around her before turning his attention back to Stella.

"You are right. As a rule Warlocks do not hold emotional attachments. However I don't happen to fall under the category of the normal Warlock. And you my child are not of normal Elf blood."

"I told you Stella. I told you he was different." Her mother said through a stream of tears. Then she turned to look up at Garrett, her face beamed. It was as if she'd forgotten the hurtful remarks from her daughter she was so captivated with this being.

That alone enforced her opinion that her mother was a traitor to the family. At that moment she loathed her mother.

"Okay, Warlock. You and that traitor that calls herself my mother can leave this family, but first tell me what makes you so different from the others?"

Now he frowned at her for this hard line she was taking. "George here," he glanced at George, "stems from the Gareg line of the Warlocks. Your mother stems from the fairy world of the Elfin line. You stem from the Fairy line as well as mine because of my mating with your mother. You see Stella, I stem from Gavin's line."

"Queen Ravena's and Prince Gareg's son?" She asked incredulously.

"The one and only," he smiled again. "He was gifted with the powers of both as are you and I."

"Are there any more of us around?"

"None that I know of. We are very unique I think."

"Good then I only have to be rid of you and not have another come at me like you have," Stella seethed.

Morgana was getting just a little nervous with Geoffrey and Wilfred so close to them. You can always count on cousin Morgana to be the sensible one.

"Maybe we can catch up on family history later. Right now," she nodded her head to the two listening in, "I think we have more serious business to attend to."

It was ridiculous how they had all forgotten about the two bound only a few feet away from them while they discussed their family lineage. But having it brought to their attention, Stella made the effort with George's help to get up off the ground and deal with the problem they had come to deal with.

Stella couldn't help the little devilment that came into her eyes. "Maybe some other time you can show me that trick with the golden rope. The one I managed awhile back doesn't even come close to the strength of yours." She would use it on him the first chance she got, was her plan.

"That would be my pleasure and you can show me how you can bring pieces of the sun into your hands."

'Oh that she was going to hang on to herself. This so called father could be full of lies and not to be trusted.' She kept those thoughts to herself.

They both laughed. The tension was gone as they turned their attention to the two quivering men standing awaiting their destiny.

With two beings possessing more power than they had ever seen, it didn't take a lot of persuasion for them to give up the location where they were holding young Stanley.

Seeing the fear in both their eyes, Stella figured a warning to them to never come at her or her family again should be enough. Geoffrey was beaten and now that he saw she possessed more power than any Warlock, she hoped he would learn from that and keep his word never to come at them again. But just to side with caution, they placed a double binding on them before allowing them to leave.

CHAPTER

Nineteen

A s they turned to leave, Stella saw Garrett accompany Wanda. She turned to them.

"I said you can leave and take that traitor with you," Stella narrowed her eyes at this stranger. She heard her mother suck in her breath at her words.

"You will not talk to your mother that way," Garrett narrowed his eyes at Stella.

"What will you do? Kill me?" Stella hissed out.

"Stella, I have no intention of doing you any harm. Your mother and I are in love, she is not a traitor. I will explain everything, but we all need to go back inside the Manor first." Garrett insisted.

"You will not dictate orders to me or any member of my family," Stella seethed at him.

"I am merely suggesting that we all sit down and talk," Garrett amended.

Wanda's kitchen was a buzz of conversation. Garrett was doing his best to field question after question being pelted at him from everyone. Now that Geoffrey and Wilfred had a double binding of their powers placed on them, they were sure not to be bothered by them for a very long time.

Stanley was found and taken to the safety of his home and sentenced to suffer the embarrassment of Naomi's constant fussing. Stella did not trust this man and kept her reflexes and alert system on high.

George didn't like the fact that he was the only one in the Manor rendered powerless. He knew now that Garrett was no immediate threat to Stella but he still felt uncomfortable without his powers.

Gwen felt a little strange. She didn't hold any grudge that Stella's father was in her life. She was happy for her sister. Nor did she have any longing to meet her father. It was just strange to have one of her mother's mates taking an interest in the family. She watched her mother glow whenever she looked at Garrett. It was very strange and very out of the ordinary.

It seemed to her that ever since her sister became what she was, everything changed in the family. Maybe it was the simple fact that the role of protective older sister wasn't needed anymore. She just knew it was going to take some time to get used the way things are now. And deep down she breathed a sigh of relief that she wasn't the chosen one to have all this new power.

Stella watched her mother and the man professing to be her father. There was definitely something there. She'd never seen her mother this way. She was acting like a young school girl with her first crush or someone put under a spell. She watched the looks that the two shot at each other. It wouldn't surprise her if they ended up together.

Trust did not come easy to her. And it hurt to know that she lost some trust in her mother as well. She still felt that her mother betrayed the family. That had her feeling that her mother was in the same category as her enemies.

With that thought she would have to decide if she liked the idea or not. But at least for now, her mother was happy and that's all that counted. She was still trying to cope with the idea that she wasn't the only one with the powers she had.

Stella still could not decide if this Garrett had her mother under a spell or not. The feeling of betrayal was still with her about her mother. That feeling will simply not go away right now.

That was a bridge she knew she would have to deal with sometime in the near future. She was thinking of having no more contact with her mother. This is something she needs to think long and hard on.

Before they left the Manor, Stella agreed for her mother's sake to think about allowing Garrett to give her away at the wedding. She knew that she had a lot of thinking to do. This man was claiming to be her father and wanting to be part of her wedding. But in the back of her mind she had no intention for him to have this honour. She was also wondering if she should have her mother at the wedding after watching her betrayal. If she banned her from the wedding this could be the first step of cutting her out of her life. Stella found she has mixed feelings about this.

Something deep inside her didn't want to trust him. He was a complete unknown to her. She was very suspicious of the way her mother acted when he was around. Again she wondered if she should exclude her own mother from the wedding. It didn't take a lot of time for her to make up her mind. Neither one will be allowed to attend the wedding. For some reason that did have her feeling a wee bit better.

As soon as they stepped outside the Manor, a storm of relief washed over George as his powers were once again freed from the confines of the spells.

Stella was still feeling the effects her transforming always caused her. She laid her head back against the headrest of the borrowed car on the drive back to Dave's office.

George drove slowly giving her time to recoup. While keeping one hand on the steering wheel, the other was busy stroking her arm. He needed the physical contact to settle his own nerves down. Never did he want to ever be that close again to believing he might lose her forever. Just thinking of it stabbed a pain in his heart.

"George I still don't know if I can trust him." She breathed out. "I don't know what power he has over my mother and the worst of it is, I don't know if I can ever trust my mother again."

"I sensed the rift between you the moment she went to him in the clearing. I'm sorry for that sweetheart."

"Yeah, I don't know what I should feel about that. I do know that I feel she betrayed us." She sighed. "George I don't want either one at our wedding."

George knew this was a decision she had to make on her own. Having her mother rush to the man she thought was going to be responsible for killing her entire family, was a huge blow for her. All he could do now was to be patient and support any decision she comes to.

George remained silent on the drive over to Dave's office, giving her time to mull it all over in her mind.

Dave watched them as they made their way into his office. 'My God,' he thought, 'they look like they've been through hell and back.' He got up from behind his desk to help George guide Stella to a chair. She was still suffering the effects. Her muscles hadn't quite firmed up yet.

He'd seen Stella in action at the theater leaping over chairs springing into the air and tackle down a suspect. He'd heard of her exploits on the force. He didn't think there was anything this strong kick-ass woman couldn't do. Now he watched her folding into a chair like a limp rag. Thankfully there were no visible marks on her to give him more cause for worry. But she looked like she'd been put through the wringer.

"My God Stella, what the hell happened?" He pushed a cup of coffee in her hands.

'Jeez,' she thought, do I look that bad?' Her arms felt like lead as she lifted her hand to rub across her face.

"Thanks," taking the cup he offered.

"We ran into a bit more than we expected," she attempted a weak laugh. "Don't worry, Dave, I'm okay, just a little tired." She told him.

"What the hell happened?" He was really worried now.

"Like Stella said," George piped up. "We ran into a bit more than expected. Stella is fine, just a bit worn out. We'll fill you in later if that's okay Dave. Right now we'd like to get back into our own clothes and rest for a bit. Are the two decoys back?"

"Yeah, they came in about a half hour ago." He wasn't convinced they were as good as they professed but seeing Stella's state, he didn't push them for more details.

After knowing Stella for a lengthy time, he knew she was always a bit of a dark horse when it came to talking about her work. He'd seen her bruised and battered and still come out of it swinging. Whatever the trouble they ran into this time must have been a hell of a lot more than she could handle.

It always bothered Dave how she kept secrets and allowed no one in. And it bothered him too to realize that George was given that privilege and not him, since he's known her much longer than him. If he didn't know better, he'd suspect she didn't trust him.

George insisted Stella rest a bit longer, long enough to finish her coffee. When she put her cup down he helped her up and with an arm around her led her down the hall to one of the rooms to change out of the decoy's clothes.

They thanked Dave again on their way out, climbed into George's car and headed back to her house.

George took her around to the back door instead of through her office. He didn't want her thinking about work right now. Her legs were a little sturdier under her now as she climbed the stairs leading up to the kitchen.

He led her down the hall to the small living room and pulled her down on the sofa with him. He could see her strength coming back as she sat tapping her fingers on her knees. He watched the frown forming on her face telling him she was going over the events in her mind.

"I wonder why it is that no one even thought about Gavin having a lineage." She still couldn't wrap her mind around the fact that this strange Warlock called himself her father. Still thinking of him, she wasn't convinced that he was the only descendant from that line.

"As far as I know there were no archives for him. The archives handed down came from the original two worlds. Gavin was only a product of those two."

"So you're saying no one thought to write down anything about Gavin's powers. If that is true, that would leave any sired from Gobrath and whatever he mated with out of the loop too." Fear trickled down her spine.

George's head snapped around. That idea had never occurred to him. Now that he was on the same page as her, he realized it was more than possible that there may be more magic, stronger magic than he possessed living among the humans.

"How long have you kept this idea to yourself?" His eyes narrowed.

"The moment Garrett told us about himself it made sense that there had to be others with different powers." She sighed.

"And you didn't deem it necessary to let me in on this?" George was growing angrier by the minute. He knew his anger stemmed from fear for her safety and the fact that he never thought of this. If what she was imagining was true, his powers would never be enough to help her. Every new development was rendering him more and more useless to her.

"George," she touched his arm hoping the contact would ease some of his tension, "It's only a theory," she tried to soften the blow he was suffering.

"Yes it's only a theory, but one that I should have thought of as well. I've been letting you down in so many ways, Stella." He felt he was more of a hindrance to her than anything else and that could cost her, her life one day.

"Stop that," she took his face in her hands and made him look at her. "You have never let me down and I don't ever want you to talk like that again. My life has changed since the day I met you. If it wasn't for you I would have gone mad. You saved me from that."

Now she looked right into his eyes her love pouring from hers to his. "I know that since I became more than anyone ever thought I would that your pride has suffered and I'm sorry for that. But I can't live this life without you. Believe me.

"George please believe me when I say I love you more than life and can't go on without you. I need you George. I need you to be with me. We'll work out the rest only if you don't leave me."

The intensity of love in her eyes and the pleading in her voice release the anger in him. Even though he thought himself more hindrance than anything else, he knew he could not live one day without her. This was his miracle sitting beside him. He would just have to live knowing the strength she needed from him wasn't his magic but his love.

George leaned over to rest his brow on hers and whispered, "I will be with you for as long as you want me. I love you beyond reason."

They spent the rest of the night showing each other the depths of their love for each other. Canada day had nothing on the fireworks that went on in her bedroom that night.

The previous weeks of stress had them both sleeping in late the next morning. They both woke feeling lighter now that they knew Geoffrey and his son were not going to be after them for a very long time.

They got out of bed to face a day filled with normal, leaving magic behind them.

While they busied themselves getting dressed then fixing breakfast, Louise was across town getting an early start on planning a bridal shower and bachelorette party for Stella. Gwen was back in her apartment getting ready for work. Wanda was spending her time at the Manor enjoying her time with Garrett.

Dr. Ballard was in his office finishing up his report on the young Jed Bonner. He hoped to God never to see that atrocity again. He sent up a silent prayer, thinking it couldn't hurt, that the Lieutenants would have the culprits responsible for the deed. It still unnerved him thinking of the two, knowing now what he did about them.

Just as he finished the file and was about to close it, a noise had him looking up to see the two he was thinking of standing in his doorway. Not being a particularly religious man, he marveled at the fact his prayer was answered so quickly.

George waited for the doctor to look up so as not to startle him.

"Doctor Ballard we'd like to speak with you if you have a minute."

Ballard motioned them in and indicated to them to take a seat. He closed the file and sat with his hands clasped on the desk.

"I've just finished up with young Mr. Bonner. I can't tell you how happy I'd be never to see that again." He raised his eyebrows at the two.

"That's what we've come to discuss with you." George spoke softly. "The people responsible will not be able to do such harm for we hope a very long time."

"I'd be happier Lieutenant had you said the word never." He glared at him.

"We are very sorry, Dr. But due to, shall we say, certain circumstances that we can't go into, nor do I think you would want us to, there can be no permanent resolution, only a temporary one."

Dr. Ballard mulled that over. They were right. He didn't want to know what the circumstances were.

"So what you are telling me is that you people have no judicial system."

Stella's lips curled up in a grin she tried to hide, while George coughed into his hand to cover his. "Let's just say we deal with things a bit differently. I can assure you that you should not have this sort of thing cross your desk for a good long time."

"Dr. Ballard," Stella spoke out. "I want to thank you again for your understanding and your word not to give us away. I am sorry that you were put in this situation, but I can't think of anyone I've trusted more."

Her words took some of the sting out of what he had agreed to do for them. He still admired her for the years of work she did on the force. To keep his feet firmly on the ground he had to believe that she was still the same person he knew before she came to him with her incredible story. Thinking of her the way she was before, helped.

"I will keep the both of you to your word that I won't have to deal with the atrocities I've had to deal with lately. Those poor bodies and their families need to have answers." Dr. Ballard told them.

They left the doctor's office knowing they had put his mind to rest of ever seeing another mutilation by magic for a long time. George dropped Stella back at her house then drove himself to headquarters to finish up some paperwork. They planned on going to the beach later for some much needed R & R.

Garrett had waited for George to leave before walking up to Stella's door. He wanted some time alone with her. It still felt very strange for him to feel this attachment he had for his offspring. The pride he felt for what he and Wanda had produced had him wanting to get to know her better.

They had a lot to learn and teach each other. Wanda had filled him in on her life. He knew in order to learn more about her he needed to earn her trust. That was the first step and he decided to start earning it now.

He walked in and waited for her to make the first move. It was up to her to invite him in or send him away. The seconds passed while he held his breath.

Stella looked up at the sound of him coming through the door. She held his stare sizing him up. She knew he would seek her out and wasn't surprised at his coming to her. Finally she gestured to him to come in and take a seat. She was as curious to find out more about him as he was to find out more about her.

Their conversation was hesitant at first each trying to feel out the other. "I've heard as a rule that Warlocks don't care about the offspring they sire. What makes me different in that area?" She asked.

"You'd be right about not taking any particular interest in the child sired. I can't explain it. I should have been content that your mother conceived and left it at that." Suddenly he began to blush.

"So why didn't you?" Stella remained suspicious.

Talking about the intimacy between Wanda and himself was a bit embarrassing especially talking about it to his daughter. Garrett coughed into his hand to try and hide the embarrassment.

"Strangely enough your mother was different somehow. I found myself having strange feelings for her. And then when I read about all your exploits on the Force and in this profession you've taken on, I was very curious to see you."

"So instead of simply knocking on my door, you decide to play tricks and worry my entire family." She threw at him.

"It was never my intention to worry any of you. I just needed to see you and to see what you've become. I'm so proud of you Stella; you have no idea how proud I am of you."

"I'm not interested in how you feel about me. Tell me why George couldn't sense you if you are a Warlock?" Stella still wasn't convinced he means no harm to her and the family.

Garrett threw back his head and surprised her by laughing.

"I don't see anything funny about it. You've made him begin to doubt himself and I want to know why." She tossed at him.

"Oh Stella, that was never my intention either. Your Warlock cannot sense me because he is from Gareg's World. I am from the Fairy World handed down through Gavin. To make it simple let's just say that our DNA is different. George can sense me only if he puts all his efforts into it. I however can sense all Warlocks."

Stella thought that one over. At least knowing that George can sense him will give him more confidence in himself.

"I've been told I'm not from Gavin, but from Ravena. How is it that we both have the same powers?" she asked.

"Stella we have the same powers along with some different ones as well. Your gifts come from the union between Royalty from the Fairy World and Warlock World. Mine come from the combination in Gavin plus his gifts as well. I will never harm you my dear. I too am from the good side of the Warlock World. And Stella, your mother means a great deal to me. I know now that she is my heart." Garrett reassured her.

That last comment shocked her. As far as she knew only Ravena and Gareg married until she agreed to marry George. Having another Warlock proclaim his love for a descendant of the Fairy World boggled her mind.

Stella didn't know what to think of that. She was also not willing to put aside the betrayal her mother displayed in the clearing.

"My mother is a traitor to our family," she stated.

"Oh my dear, you don't know how much that pains me to hear you think that. She is so very hurt that you think that of her."

"She risked our whole family by allowing you in again," Stella needed to remain firm on this point.

"Stella, all I can say is that something special, something different happened when we met and mated. I had never felt this way towards any other Elfin blood before and never engaged in mating with another since her." Garrett explained.

"So you have mated with others and in doing so there can be more of what we are." Stella said as the fear of that thought grew inside her.

That gave pause to Garrett. He'd not heard of another like him or his daughter in all these years through all his travels. This possibility did have him worry a bit now, but he didn't want to cause her more worry at this time. She brought up a point that he hadn't thought of as yet.

The two of them hedged around a bit more with questions and answers. But soon they learned to throw caution to the wind and got down to really talking to each other. Stella wanted to learn more about this Warlock. Garrett told her of some of his exploits while Stella told him simple stories of her time on the force. Soon they were laughing and talking like a couple of old friends. Although the conversation turned light, Garrett sensed her unwillingness to change her mind towards him and her mother and that too worried him.

Being a member of the Force for so many years, she used that training to make him think she was coming around, while all the time she got him to tell her more about himself.

It was never his intent to come between mother and daughter. Now he knows that it was the way he went about trying to keep a secretive eye on his daughter that caused this. Garrett knew he has to fix the rift his actions caused between them.

"Stella, I can only apologize for the way I went about trying to find out about you that caused you so much concern and fear. Your mother and I found a very special bond between us, which was a tremendous surprise to the both of us. Please don't think badly or blame your mother for my actions of trying to find a way to approach you." He begged her.

Stella sat back and thought about all that he said.

"I don't know you. Yes, the way you tried to find a way to find out about me put me on full alert, but now that we have met, I will need time." She didn't give in lightly.

"I hope that we can come to terms with this situation." Garrett stated.

"I have lost one career that I loved, I will not tolerate you or my mother in ending this career that I've chosen and have come to enjoy." She warned him.

"I'm sorry that you felt your mother is the cause of ending one, but I can assure you that I will never do anything to interfere with the path you have now chosen." He vowed to her.

"Oh you can be very sure I will not tolerate any actions by my mother to end this career." She glared at him. "Should I sense any chance of her ruining what I have now, I will end my relationship with her forever. You can tell the traitor what I just said."

"Stella, please I do beg of you not to think so harshly of her. She didn't know you would take her actions as traitorous. She just can't help showing what is in her heart. She loves you with every fiber of her being." Garrett pled Wanda's case.

"You can beg all you want Warlock, but you will not tell me what to do or how to feel." She warned him.

"I did not come here to tell you anything, but to explain to you how your mother and I feel about each other. I only wanted to meet you to get to know you better. I hope that I can earn your trust." He told her.

"You're right in one thing, trust has to be earned." Stella decided to keep her distance emotionally from him for now. She realized it will be useless and maybe fatal to anger this Warlock since she doesn't know what all he's capable of yet.

Garrett sensed what was in her mind and sat back and relaxed a bit.

They talked for a long time and when it was time for him to leave, Stella sensed they would both be in each other's lives from then on.

Stella wasn't sure how she felt about having him in her life yet. This she was going to take one day at a time until he proved himself to her. As for her mother, she knew it was going to take longer to ever truly trust her again. She still was of two minds whether to allow her to take part in her wedding.

Stella had made up her mind a long time ago to have Shawn Riley give her away on her wedding. He was a real father figure to her. She still wants him to have that honour. She doesn't know this Garrett person well enough to usurp Shawn from this honour. To her, Shawn was more of a father than this stranger that's just come into her life.

CHAPTER

Twenty

D ebra and Angela were busy in Debra's home studio. Deb was busy designing the bride's maid and maid of honour dresses for Stella's wedding. Angela was at her desk going over some of the details for Debra's next fashion show.

The only sounds in the room were Angela's soft sighs over the impossible task of creating the venue for her boss's inventive imagination and Debra humming as she sketched out designs.

Richard heaved his own sigh as he looked into the room on his way to get a coffee. The love of his life was happily in her zone. For now she was safe, but how long would that last, he wondered? Being friends with Stella Blake was very dangerous and he just couldn't relax not knowing when the next time Debra would be facing danger again.

He shrugged shaking his head and turned to take the stairs down to the kitchen. As he walked he realized that as long as Deb remained stubborn wanting to stay where she is, he'd have to do something about soundproofing his work room. Leaving for his cottage up north to do his writing was quite out of the question now.

Because of the many cancellations over the break-in at her office, Gwen found she had time today to go over to her mother's and help with the wedding plans.

It did cut deep that her clients felt they couldn't trust her. All she could do was to apologize to them and tell them that it would never happen again as she has found a safe place to keep all her files and records where no one can access them.

Some of her patients were willing to give her another chance, but there were a few that would never come back to her again. The Senator was one of them.

Once everyone was gathered in the kitchen it didn't take long for all the chatter to be focused on Stella's special day. Louise was only too happy to tell them about the shower and bachelorette party. That had them all squealing with delight.

The other night's business was forgotten as they all dived in with their own particular ideas they wanted implemented in the events. With all the excitement and trying to talk over each other, none of them noticed Morgana sitting, not saying a word, with a scowl on her face.

Wanda too was not showing the enthusiasm she should be. Her daughter's parting remarks to her still resonated with her. Until then, she never knew it was she that ruined her daughter's career on the Force. Then to have her daughter tell her she is a traitor cut her very deeply.

In Morgana's mind, Stella getting married was pish-posh and a lot of senselessness. She was a firm believer in doing things the way they were always done. Mate with a Warlock and then walk away from him. She found women to be weak that felt they needed a man about the house on a constant basis.

Morgana was especially disturbed over the way her cousin was acting towards this Warlock that claims to have fathered Stella. Of course in her mind, Wanda was always a bit flighty in the brain to begin with. Now her scowl was directed straight at Wanda.

Normally Gwen would send waves of calm out to soothe her cousin, but this time she felt her mother should deal with the formidable cousin on her own. She too was not convinced of this Garrett's sincerity. She sided with her sister on this issue.

It didn't happen often, but this time she was on her sister's side of things when it came to their mother's strange behavior towards a Warlock none of them knew until now. She had her doubts and worries for her mother's safety and sanity and the safety of the family.

Gwen decided last night in the clearing that she would keep her eye on both this Warlock and her mother. Her gift can warn her sister if and when she felt danger from him.

Louise was blissfully unaware of the thoughts going on inside the minds of the other women. She was bouncing with excitement over the planning of the events.

While all the women were gathered for planning events for Stella, George sat in his office quietly going over in his head the events of last night.

He'd reached for the phone at least a half dozen times to call her and just hear her voice telling him she was alright. But he knew her too well and knew she would be very angry with him thinking she wasn't strong enough to handle things herself.

George didn't realize that he snapped at his team when they came into his office to discuss their cases. They sat at their desks in the squad room looking at each other.

The whole team looked to Tom as their unofficial leader. All he could do was shrug and shake his head at them. He had no idea what has put their Lieutenant in such a foul mood today.

"It's probably something personal. I think we should just try to stay out of his way for awhile and give him time to sort it all out." He suggested to the others.

Sally wasn't so sure Tom was right, but gave him the benefit of the doubt and agreed to his suggestion. She knew firsthand what a family argument can be like. If Tom was right, and it was family related, he'd sort it out. All families do eventually. So she agreed and got busy with her work.

The first thing Stella did after Garrett left was to call Naomi and find out how she was doing. She needed to know that the young genius brother of hers wasn't suffering too badly after his ordeal.

"Oh Miss Blake, I don't know how I can ever thank you. You saved Stanley's life, again."

"No need for thanks Naomi, I was just doing my job. I only called to see if he was doing okay." She told her.

"Well, um," she hesitated. "I don't think he's suffering any ill effects, not physically anyway. But," she coughed to hide her embarrassment.

"But," Stella sat straight up in her chair. "Naomi, does he need medical attention? Or if he's having a hard time because of his experience, I can recommend my sister to take him on as a patient." Stella was worried the young man was suffering mental afflictions from his ordeal.

"Um, thanks, but no," Naomi paused again. "I don't know how to say this, but Stanley tells me I'm hovering and it's making him uncomfortable. But oh, Miss Blake, I can't help it, I love him and what happened to him scares me so much. He wants me to back off. Those were his words. He says I'm smothering him."

Stella heard her crying softly over the phone.

Well the little entrepreneur had more spunk in him than she thought he did, she smiled to herself.

"Naomi, it sounds like he is suffering no ill effects, maybe you should give him a little space. If you go around worried all the time about him, it just may upset him and then he'd be worried about you."

Guilt was always a good tool to use.

"Oh, oh yes you're right. I don't want him to worry for a minute about me or anything."

"There, that's the spirit. Okay, now that I know the two of you are going to be fine, I have to get back to work." Stella could only handle so much whimpering at the moment.

"Of course and thank you Miss Blake, thank you for everything."

Stella hung up sensing a slight headache brewing. To take her mind off of the last few days, we reached over and pulled out the files from her inbox. She needed to concentrate on something other than the magic overload she just endured.

It had been a very busy few weeks. So much had happened around and to her. Stella marveled at the fact that she didn't lose her mind. The most amazing part was that she actually accepted who and what she is now. But the most incredible part was that she knew she had more to learn about herself and that George was going to be with her by her side on this most fantastic journey.

Getting married still made her edgy and nervous, but now she knew she could face that knowing it will tie her and George together for the rest of their lives.

That happy thought stayed with her as she pulled out the files and began reading through them. Even knowing that the RCMP and especially Inspector Wise was still keeping a close eye on her did not dampen her little happy mood.

That's how George found her after work, humming away as she jotted down notes in her notebook.

There she sat his personal miracle. After all that happened today and leading up to today, she can sit there humming. He walked over and watched as she turned and stared up at him.

"Is it any wonder I love you so much," he smiled down at her. All the tension and anger took wing and flew away. Just one look at her had the self doubting lifted away. The anger he felt from being proved less powerful than Stella and this man claiming to be her father seemed inconsequential now.

"It's a good thing since I happen to love you too." Her voice turned husky.

Those words were all it took for him to lift her out of the chair and take her up the stairs to her private quarters and into the bedroom. He wiggled his fingers to lock up her office before heading up the stairs.

Now all he wanted to do was to show her how very much he loves her. All Stella wanted to do was to show him she didn't love him for what flows in their veins but what fills her heart.

That night her bedroom was filled with soft sprays of light and heat. Their lovemaking was so sweet and tender it caused tears to fill their eyes at what each gave to the other.

The trip to the beach would have to wait for another day. Soft sand and warm breezes could never come close to making them feel more tuned in and relaxed as a night of passion does.

Proving their love chased all thoughts of danger away. For tonight neither one thought about family or magic, except for the magic they brought to each other.

They both allowed the fantasy of thinking all was well and trouble was the thing of the past. And for a few hours they were right.

It was just too bad that other magic lurking in their near future wasn't feeling the same or the love.

Garrett knew that the daughter he sired still does not trust him and that she is now angry with her mother. This is something he knows he has to work on. Hopefully he can learn more about his daughter through Wanda. What hurts his love hurts him.

It has surprised him to learn that his daughter has fought what is in her all her life and is just now finding out what flows in her veins. He now feels that it will be up to him to teach and train her for the role she has been ordained to fill.

He has known his entire life what he is. Finding a mate that filled his heart with love was a shock to him at first. Now he only wishes to remain with his love and to teach their offspring how to utilize all her powers. But after talking with his daughter he now realizes that he will have to find a way for her to trust him. Trust has to be earned and he'll need to earn it to become a solid member of this family.